Stories by Contemporary W

Gone with the
River Mist

This book is edited and designed by the Editorial Committee of *Cultural China* series

Text by Yao Emei
Translation by Jiang Yajun
Cover Image by Getty Images
Interior Design by Xue Wenqing
Cover Design by Wang Wei

Assistant Editor: Cao Xiaoying
Editors: Yang Xiaohe, Kirstin Mattson
Editorial Director: Zhang Yicong

Senior Consultants: Sun Yong, Wu Ying, Yang Xinci
Managing Director and Publisher: Wang Youbu

ISBN: 978-1-60220-250-4

Address any comments about *Gone with the River Mist* to:

Better Link Press
99 Park Ave
New York, NY 10016
USA

or

Shanghai Press and Publishing Development Company
F 7 Donghu Road, Shanghai, China (200031)
Email: comments_betterlinkpress@hotmail.com

Printed in China by Shanghai Donnelley Printing Co., Ltd.

1   3   5   7   9   10   8   6   4   2

Gone with the River Mist

By Yao Emei

Better Link Press

Foreword

This collection of books for English readers consists of short stories and novellas published by writers based in Shanghai. Apart from a few who are immigrants to Shanghai, most of them were born in the city, from the latter part of the 1940s to the 1980s. Some of them had their works published in the late 1970s and the early 1980s; some gained recognition only in the 21st century. The older among them were the focus of the "To the Mountains and Villages" campaign in their youth, and as a result, lived and worked in the villages. The difficult paths of their lives had given them unique experiences and perspectives prior to their eventual return to Shanghai. They took up creative writing for different reasons but all share a creative urge and a love for writing. By profession, some of them are college professors, some literary editors, some directors of literary institutions, some freelance writers and some professional writers. From the individual styles of the authors and the art of their writings, readers can easily detect traces of the authors' own experiences in life, their interests, as well as their aesthetic values. Most of the works in this collection are still written in the realistic style that represents, in a painstakingly fashioned fictional world, the changes of the times in urban and rural life. Having grown up in a more open era, the younger writers have been spared the hardships experienced by their predecessors, and therefore seek greater freedom in their writing. Whatever category of writers they belong to, all of them have gained their rightful places in Chinese literary circles over the last forty years. Shanghai writers tend to favor urban narratives more than other genres of writing. Most of the works in this collection can be characterized as urban literature with Shanghai characteristics, but there are also exceptions.

Called the "Paris of the East," Shanghai was already an international metropolis in the 1920s and 30s. Being the center of China's economy, culture and literature at the time, it housed a majority of writers of importance in the history of modern Chinese literature. The list includes Lu Xun, Guo Moruo, Mao Dun and Ba Jin, who had all written and published prolifically in Shanghai. Now, with Shanghai re-emerging as a globalized metropolis, the Shanghai writers who have appeared on the literary scene in the last forty years all face new challenges and literary quests of the times. I am confident that some of the older writers will produce new masterpieces. As for the fledging new generation of writers, we naturally expect them to go far in their long writing careers ahead of them. In due course, we will also introduce those writers who did not make it into this collection.

Wang Jiren
Series Editor

Chapter One

A schoolgirl looked up from her map of China, which she had been reading for quite a while.

"I think the Yangtze River looks more like a centipede, and the rivers and streams that mingle with it on their way to the sea are its legs," she told her teacher. A ripple of laughter immediately ran through the classroom.

The teacher stood still for a moment and then nodded understandingly. "That comparison doesn't sound as nice but it's a unique one." The girl responded with a smile. She had learned from her books that the Yangtze River was like a huge dragon, but she had never seen a dragon. She knew what a centipede was.

The girl was Ma Xiaoyu, Ma being her surname from her maternal grandmother, and Xiaoyu meaning "Little Yu." She was not abashed by the laughter of her classmates, and she buried herself again in the map, trying to find the leg of her centipede named for the Wuhe River, literally "river of mist." She searched for a long time until her eyes blurred, but in vain.

She came to her teacher again. "You think the Wuhe River is mighty but it is tiny on a map, so much so that it is not marked," she was told. Little Yu didn't see why such a large river, which provided water for the whole town of Wuluo (meaning "fall of mist"), could be considered so insignificant as to be ignored.

If the river was not marked, what about the town? She went

to the map again right away, and nowhere could she see the name of Wuluo.

It is true that the Wuhe River is a large one, surrounded by many stories. Legend has it that a fish in the river cried like a baby during the night, putting a magic spell on the women so that they left their own babies while they were feeding, and ran to the river to see what was happening. It was a long time ago, in ancient times, and the fish has never been seen—an old legend for an old river.

As for the source of the river, several competing theories exist. When it appears as a small shallow stream, and looks like a loose thread from a distance, some people claim it rises from a mountain spring near their village. When the spring dries up, the river runs dry. It may become muddy yellow overnight in some seasons, and winds like a boa constrictor, overflowing its banks to ruin the crops and the farmland.

Some people claim it has its source in the heavens. It was said that three huge columns of water appeared on a mountain. They rose above the clouds, and the sound of the roaring water could be heard more than a hundred miles away, as if thunder.

However the river is quiet most of the time. A breeze may ripple the surface, making it spark as if a river of mercury. Several herb collectors coming back from a trip into the mountains once told the villagers that the Wuhe River ran out of a cave in the remote peaks, revealing what they had discovered on their journey.

When asked where the water in the cave came from, a shrewd man stood out from the crowd and said, "You know what? Three-fourths of the earth's surface is water. As the waters on earth are connected, you may see the sea when you go all the way into the cave."

No one in the crowd would want to attempt this, of course, because they thought his theory was simply groundless. They burst out laughing, wondering at thought that the earth is covered with more water than land. There must be more land, something they could feel under their feet, because they saw much less water around them.

Years later, this wise man entered the water with a homemade wooden raft when the biggest flood in a century struck the area, thinking he would be lucky enough to reach the sea through the connected waters, only to find he had washed ashore in a place named Wuluo. Working for a shipyard afterward, he lost his enthusiasm for the sea when he learned that it took only half a month to sail out into the sea, in a ship they built, safely and securely. And later he was to end up in the water himself, as he lost control and fell into the depths, like a piece of iron, as he was trying to catch fish and shrimp in the Wuhe River. His fishing basket continued traveling east with the waves, as if nothing had happened.

He left behind in the town of Wuluo a wife, Ma Gu, who was ten years older than he, two daughters, and a granddaughter, Little Yu, the girl who compared the Yangtze River to a centipede.

A loud hammering sound was heard in the Ma house when it was still dark. Everyone in the village knew it was the last day of the month, whether the thirtieth or thirty-first, when Ma Gu's feet pained, as always, and her daughters and granddaughter accompanied her to the hospital.

A bamboo deckchair was being assembled by fastening a bamboo rod, as thick as the arm of a man and as long as three meters, to the armrest on each side. It was not an easy job and it took the inept daughters and granddaughter nearly an hour to get the rods in place.

When everything was ready, the three of them began to gather at the table for their breakfast. Ma Gu was not eating, as she had her only meal of the day at noon. Sitting to the side, she examined with great interest the deckchair and the red flannelette blanket spread out on it, wondering at how much it resembled a traditional wedding sedan chair in which a bride was carried to her new home.

At eight o'clock, when the early morning mist had cleared,

the deckchair was placed before the gate. Ma Gu rejected the help offered by the two daughters and went to sit on the chair herself, placing her feet on a transverse bar. She was unemotional and did not speak a word, either because her feet hurt or because she was enjoying the special treatment.

It was not hot but Ma Gu put her floral parasol up. Kneeling down the bearers shouted, "One, two, three!" in one voice, and the old deckchair ascended and began to move with a creaking sound. The younger daughter, Ah-Shui, was in the front and the other, Ah-Shan, was in the rear. Little Yu, Ah-Shan's daughter, walked along on one side, carrying Ma Gu's old tea pot, which had a long, angled spout, in her hand. For years her grandmother had eaten only one meal a day, but she had to drink a little green tea from her teapot every half hour.

Long ago Ma Gu learned from a lay Buddhist that the food a person would consume during a lifetime was a defined amount, determined back on the day of birth. Every meal was a reduction from the total. When the given amount was finished, one was doomed to die.

How can one survive when one has nothing to eat? Her daughters were born when she was already older, but she didn't want them left without a mother when they were still quite young. She hoped to extend her life as long as possible, and the only way she could think of was to reduce the amount of food she ate daily.

In the first days, she sat a meter away from the dining table, feeling a great sense of pride as she listened to her daughters and granddaughter munching their way through their meals and watched their lips moving like petals, while she was starving with her own stomach rumbling. Instead of telling them the truth, she told them that eating her supper would leave her sleepless at night, as she was suffering from a stomach problem. As time went on her stomach no longer rumbled at suppertime, and she lost her desire for breakfast and supper, and finally, for food.

At the same time, she found herself obsessed with a new hobby: cooking for others. When still a girl, she was forced by her mother-in-law to cook for the whole family. She was cursed and beaten when her mother-in-law was not happy about her work. The more she was abused, the more progress she made in her cooking skills.

Gradually, cooking became everything for her, and she was known as an excellent cook more than anything else. Her professionalism went beyond most people's imagination. She could create delicious meals from any plant or animal, including green bristlegrass, sparrows and even ants. She neither needed an apron nor to cover or roll up her sleeves, as many others did, to keep her clothes dry and clean when she worked. She could slice carrots, cucumbers, tofu and rice cake in her hand instead of on a chopping block. She could crack an egg with one hand. She used her hands instead of a spatula to flip pancakes in a heated pan. Her clothes would be free from stains when breakfast or dinner was ready on the kitchen table waiting for the family to enjoy. She then would sit on a chair away from the table, after washing her hands and tidying her hair, with her deep-set eyes in her pinched face moving from one person's mouth to another.

Her family had gotten used to this odd behavior, but guests would be too embarrassed to enjoy the food under her gaze, instead choosing to rush through the meal, or to ask her again and again to join them, uncomfortable as if they were sitting amongst thorns. She would refuse without exception, which would often lead to a noisy argument during otherwise quiet enjoyment.

When the last person stood up from the table, with a contented smile on her face she would begin to clear the table. Ah-Shui wondered why her mother, who did not enjoy any food, was unbelievably enthusiastic about washing up, and also how a person could resist the desire for food. She observed her without her awareness, thinking she would be picking through the leftovers to relieve her hunger. However Ma Gu didn't do this; in her eyes the food before her was an object no different than the chopping block and knives in the kitchen.

The pain in Ma Gu's feet was so strange that for a time her family thought she was only pretending. Her feet appeared no different than before—neither red nor swollen—but she complained of the pain. The doctors had no idea what was wrong with them. Most importantly she would be a totally different person after the visit to the doctor, no longer the woman who was groaning painfully before they left, but appearing robust and healthy, and looking around in all directions as they traveled. The family suspected that her only purpose was to enjoy the trip on the deckchair.

They decided to test if the pain was real. What happened was a dreadful shock to them. As usual Ma Gu was on the bed crying painfully for help. When she saw the deckchair was not coming, she began to toss her head from side to side on the pillow, and the hair she wore in a bun came loose like tangles of seaweed.

The family thought it was because of the pain in her feet before they realized that she was apoplectic with rage: she kicked away the painkiller in Ah-Shan's hand, upset a nice cup of tea that Ah-Shui prepared for her, and gritted her teeth when Little Yu offer her a piece of sweet soft rice cake, her all-time favorite.

With her eyes stitched shut and her brows furrowed, she conveyed that she would never give up. Every one of her groans was accompanied by a shiver of unease in the three women. When an expression of fear crossed Ah-Shan's face, Ah-Shui shook her head to disagree. The three women then agreed to help Ma Gu make a change in her behavior, which they still felt was fake. Anyway it was rather a hard job for a family without a man in any of its three generations to carry her in a deckchair for the trip to the hospital.

All of a sudden, Ma Gu calmed down, breathing gently, mouth open. When the three women looked at each other in amazement, thinking she had gotten over it, Ma Gu screamed, "I need an iron wire!"

Little Yu then rushed to the balcony, where their surplus items—plastic bags, hemp ropes, wall sockets, light bulbs, packaging tapes—were kept for use in an emergency. She picked a length of iron wire and handed it to her grandmother, when she was sure it was thoroughly clean.

Right away Ma Gu put the wire around her neck, and began to twist it under her chin as quickly as she could. As she gasped for breath, Ah-Shui was quick enough to move over to hold her hands still, stopping her from twisting the wire. Ma Gu was not struggling any more but her face was already like a large purple eggplant.

Ma Gu won. Things happened as they had before. On the last day of every month, before she woke up in the morning, the three women began to assemble the bamboo deckchair, make a new pot of tea, and prepare breakfast. When the clock said eight o'clock, the whole family would be dressed up as if it were a holiday, ready for the trip under the new sun.

When they walked through a crowded bazaar on their way, the shoppers would take a step back, leaving them enough space to get by. The gray-haired Ma Gu lay on the scarlet blanket on the deckchair, pointing from time to time with her bamboo stick, which was treated with tung oil to be smoother and firmer.

"Little Yu, let me have a look at that; what's this—I've never seen it before." Every time she pointed to an item, Ah-Shan and Ah-Shui had to stop for Little Yu to pick it up for her. What she liked included food, small colorful scarves and headpieces.

"Old hag, you're crazy for things that girls love. Do you know how old you are?" Ah-Shui murmured to herself. As she stopped speaking, Ah-Shui received a blow on her head from her mother's stick. Ma Gu may have had wobbly teeth but she could hear and see very well.

After injections of two drugs whose names they would never know, Ma Gu would feel much relieved as well as happier. Back home she would get off her deckchair and rush to the kitchen immediately after she returned her umbrella to its place, in order to prepare her delight as a chef: mixed congee, a porridge made by boiling a variety of beans in water. No one knew how she managed to get all the green beans, red beans, yellow beans, black beans, kidney beans, lentils and other beans whose names were unknown. Little Yu once counted her beans, and found there were as many as a dozen types.

Ma Gu had a wonderful sense of timing. She brought water with some beans to a boil, but added others when the water was already boiling. Still some she fried before they were boiled in water. She left the beans to simmer for several hours. When she uncovered the pot, a rich, delicious smell filled her nostrils. The thick porridge was pleasantly sweet and left a refreshing taste in the mouth.

Everyone in the family had to take a bath and freshen up each time before the congee was served, along with carefully chosen dim sum and a mixed fruit salad, rather than dishes containing meat. The table manners were strict, including sitting bolt upright and not slurping. The women had no idea when they had first been served the congee or for how many years they had been enjoying it.

One day Little Yu had the idea that the food was related to the pains in her grandmother's feet. "Why do you have to eat the congee when you come back from the hospital?" she asked. "Is it a desire of your mouth or your feet?"

With a piece of rice cake in her hand, Ma Gu said to herself, as if she was not listening to Little Yu, "I know it is best to be among a group of women. Do you think we would enjoy these foods with a man sitting at our table? They're only crazy about meat and wine. They don't touch dishes that only contain vegetables."

Ma Gu's young husband had been this type of man. In fact he died from his desire for fish. It was a summer day, when the river was filling up, and abundant fish and shrimp were seen in the water. He wanted to fish for their next meal. With a basket in his hand, he rushed impulsively to the river, but retuned after a few minutes to tell his wife to prepare more garlic and vinegar before he continued. He would eat the shrimp alive.

When Ma Gu was still crushing the garlic, she heard loud voices coming from the river. Her husband, who had frequently worked in the water ever since he was a boy, got a cramp in his leg immediately after he dove into the river. He drowned before he saw any fish.

It was Ma Gu who carried his wet body back home. She refused a man who offered to help by pushing him so hard that he reeled backward. She removed the weeds from his hair and nostrils, and made his clothes neat before she put her hands around his body and whispered, "Go home with me. There's a good boy."

With a sudden burst of effort she lifted him. She had never thought he could be so light, as light as he had been when she first lifted him many years before. She had come to live with his family when he was a four-year-old, wearing blue homemade clothes with a bib that was always wet with saliva and had a stinking smell. She had washed his feet for him every night before she carried him to bed. He was so light that with her hands under his arms she could easily lift him up over her head.

She could still recall that he smelled of any food he had eaten. Now his body had the odor of fish or shrimp, but he hadn't gotten the fish of which he had dreamed. She put his body into a coffin that she borrowed, and rushed to the river with a ladle in her hand. She wanted to catch some fish for him before she had the time to cry. She knew he would never get to rest if he missed out on what he wanted to eat. It came to pass that she saw a ladle full of fish and shrimp when she took it out of water. They lay motionless against one another as if they had been waiting for her.

For the next three years, Ma Gu followed the tradition of serving her husband his share of food at the table, as if he were still alive with her. She did this as if he was late for a meal and was on the way. Most of the time she would have meat or fish in his bowl, and when she ran out of meat and fish, she would prepare tofu by frying or deep-frying it in oil, or boiling it, the way meat was cooked.

She was fervent about the ritual of touching his bowl to be sure that his spirit had been with her. When the bowl was warm on one side, she knew he had been there eating; when it was not, she would worry because it meant he had not come back home for the meal and would therefore go hungry. She knew well that he was a curious man, and that he would have an even stronger sense of curiosity in the other world. When he did not return home, it was because he would have been so attracted by something he had never seen before that he had forgotten about his meal.

On the third anniversary of his death, she invited a couple of priests who performed religious rituals for her husband for a whole night. The next morning she removed his set of cutlery and his chair, which had been there for three years now. At the same time, she started a massive clean-up operation by sweeping up all items in her house belonging to men, as if she was dealing with garbage, and setting them on fire. She intended to leave nothing in the house that would make him think of the family, and nothing that would make them think of him. "The dead and the living must go their own ways, and he's comfortably dead," she thought. "But the girls have to struggle for their life, and their future can never be ruined simply because of his death."

She asked Ah-Shui, who was not at that time with the family, to come back home, and told Little Yu that she should never move out before she got married. She wanted the family to be as close to one another as they could be.

She announced, as the head of the house, that a family was a family, and no one was allowed to go her own way for her own self-interest without considering the needs of the family. As every new leader does, she changed some rules to quickly make an impact. Among her measures was her beating of Little Yu, who lingered in her room while others were at the dining table having their meals, but came out like a cat searching for food when they finished.

"This relates to more than when one eats; it shows a disrespect for others," Ma Gu said.

"But I need respect too. Do you think you respect me when you force me to eat when I don't feel like eating?" Little Yu replied defiantly.

Her grandmother was surprised by the challenge. "You mention my respect for you when you don't know what you're doing?" She raised her hand to hit Little Yu before she finished her words.

Little Yu liked scarves, and she was never seen without one around her neck. No one in the family noticed the special fondness of hers initially, but when they did she had more scarves in her closet than any other clothes.

Some believed that it was because her neck was so long that she needed a scarf to cover part of it. Little Yu was rather thin and tall, like the green bamboos on the hills. Others thought it was because she was so lonely that she needed a scarf's company, with its two ends moving around her when she walked. She was always by herself and was never seen with anyone else. Strangely enough, while those stripped to the waist might look uncomfortably hot in high summer, Little Yu brought with her a feeling of a light breeze, with her thin scarf hanging loosely over her shoulders.

Little Yu worked for a store selling household goods, but her secret plan was to wait until she had some money, with which she would leave the small town surrounded by hills to finish her school education. She was sure the money was on its way to her, and what she had to do was to wait for half a year, or a month, or just another day.

She worked with two older shop assistants, who preferred

sitting in a corner twittering about their family trifles while preparing vegetables for cooking (they always brought their own vegetables to the store to trim), leaving her to serve the customers behind the counter. Their topics were nothing more than what meals to have today or tomorrow, whose son was to get married and whose father was to celebrate his birthday, whose husband came home and woke her up for sex, and whose husband left her alone for a month so she slept well.

Little Yu often stood behind the counter with a magazine that had beautiful girls on the cover in front of her. It was usually a back copy that she had read numerous times. The customers were often middle-aged women. Little Yu stood emotionless as she watched them comb through the items endlessly, wondering what they were looking for. They were the very same things to her, but still the women hesitated after tapping them in their hand, listening to the noise they made, and examining them through narrowed eyes under the light, as if they were experts.

Extremely bored, Little Yu averted her eyes from them to think about the scarf she was knitting. She had to have a scarf with her, and she could never move a step without one around her neck. Once on her way back from a trip to a kiln for goods, her scarf blew away into the river. They were in a motorboat so it didn't stop for her to get her scarf back. She was so embarrassed that she covered her neck with her arms as if trying to hide her naked body. Finally an idea came to her, and she moved her coat up around her neck. Standing against the chilly breeze without outerwear, she got cold and was not able to go to work for the next three days.

Sometimes Little Yu would turn her eyes to the hill behind the houses. It was Five-Peak Mountain, the five peaks providing a backdrop for the town, as if it were a small piece of cobblestone buried in a prickly bush. Legend said this small town was the one where the Dhyani Buddha helped the Tang dynasty Buddhist monk Xuanzang to train the Monkey King. This was on his legendary pilgrimage to the Dahila Kingdom of India to obtain Buddhist sacred texts. The five peaks were believed to be the fingers and thumb of the Dhyani Buddha, whose hands could be as large as he wanted them to be. It was with this skill of his that he tamed the Monkey King, a monkey born from a stone nourished by the Five Elements of Gold, Wood, Water, Fire and Earth.

Like the vast majority of people in the town, Little Yu had never been beyond the hill, as it was almost impossible to travel to the other side. Block-shaped, with its sheer cliffs shrouded in mist all year round, it was a hill to be seen nowhere else in the world.

Passenger buses had to rumble all the way up the hill to the top and then down the other side, and the drivers had to deal with seventy-two sharp turns with great care on each side. Under the windows of each bus were remains of vomit from sick passengers. Local people usually watched with a feeling of sympathy the buses coming from outside and the pale travelers who were too sick to speak. All those many turns would make people who had never gotten sick on a bus want to vomit.

"Why is the town in the middle of five peaks?" Little Yu wondered. But at second thought, she realized that there would be no Wuluo—no "town of mist"—if the peaks were not there. They blocked the sunlight and kept the town covered in a thick gray mist.

Ma Gu was not happy about Little Yu, her granddaughter, who kept to herself, with lidded eyes and a scarf around her neck, but there was nothing she could do about her. Little Yu had been lonely and quiet ever since she was a small girl. She would skip rope alone under a wall when other kids played noisily as a group. She was shy but stubborn.

"There's nothing wrong with your neck, so why do you cover it up?" Ma Gu once asked while pulling the scarf from Little Yu's shoulder. Without a word, her granddaughter reached her hand out until her scarf was returned.

Another time she was pleased to see, for the first time ever, that her granddaughter was going out to the vegetable market without her scarf, after she washed her hair. As she was smiling to herself, Little Yu came back for her scarf.

"Do you think you would die without that?" she spat.

"You wouldn't die without your clothes on, so why do you wear them?" Little Yu challenged.

Her grandmother stood in amazement in the middle of the room, unable to speak a word.

Chapter Two

People in Wuluo had never had any idea what the morning glow and the evening glow were. The town was always shrouded in a thick blanket of fog before sunrise and after sunset, and nothing even one meter away was visible. So the townspeople were in the bad habit of going to bed early and rising late. They had nothing to do but stay at home, waiting anxiously for the fog to lift. If they were not patient enough, they had to feel their way around outside with the help of a flashlight. In the foggy town, no season was an off season for flashlights, which were available in all stores. Even food or clothing stores were seen with a sign outside, scrawled with "Flashlights."

Once a man was carrying a large piece of glass to use in his home. A dense mist came down and covered everything as he was still on his way, because he had miscalculated how long the trip would take. He blustered his way through the crowds along the street, until he ran into a lost goat standing at the roadside. The panic-stricken goat jumped up and the man was knocked down. The glass that he had been carrying for almost a whole day dropped on the ground and broke into pieces, just when he was approaching his home. To make it even worse, he nearly lost his right toe.

It puzzled the local people for quite a long time, when hearing a pupil, sitting on top of a courtyard wall, recite the lesson for the day, "… A red sun is rising on the horizon at six o'clock …"

They had never seen the sun rising at six o'clock. At that time it was still pitch-dark or the town was enveloped in a thick blanket of mist. Nor did they know what the horizon was. The earliest they saw the sun was at eight, after the mist cleared by mid-morning, and it was a yellowish disk on the top of the mist-soaked hill to the east. Years later, when a local person was at a theater and saw stage fog for the first time, he thought about the mist back home. He wondered if it was a god who blew huge fog rings down onto his town.

After the mist lifted, the stone paths were wet and the cobblestones on them were as clean as washed eggs. In this sunless, misty place, the faces of women were dewy too, and the bangs hanging on their foreheads grew darker with damp. Like shade-loving plants, they were busty, plump and fair complexioned.

Ma Gu was younger at the time, without a single gray hair on her head. As her daughters were turning into grown women, she searched every store for cloth in colors other than blue, black and dark red, but in vain. She hated the blue and black dresses they wore. Nor was she pleased with their red ones because she thought red had to do with blood, which went against one of her superstitions.

As usual she locked herself up in a room with closed curtains, leaving herself alone with her secret: meditating in the dark. The two daughters learned about this secret custom as time passed, calling it "trick playing," a name they used for anything they failed to understand. When they saw the door was locked and the curtains pulled back, they knew her mother was about to "play tricks." They were not allowed to disturb her or ask her what she had done in the room.

To learn more about their mother's secret, they took turns looking through a hole they had made in the door. They knelt on the ground for half an hour, but to their disappointment, all their mother had done was to sit still with her head lowered, as if she were sleeping. They also noticed the detail that her hand was seldom free or still. What she had in her hand was probably her medium, the means by which she communicated with something invisible, they thought. This time it was a piece of vivid yellow cloth with red flowers on it, a nice handkerchief she had picked up on her way.

When all was done, she pushed the door open, looking like a different woman, as if she had been woken from a beauty sleep. As suggested in her meditation, she went out to the hill with a small basket in her hand. She came home with some purple fruits, green vines, yellow leaves and red flowers, which she carefully put into a pot in a certain order. After pouring in thirty-six gourds of water, she boiled the mixture for three hours, until it turned into a pot of blue ink. She then put into the liquid two of her daughters' dresses, one for each. With the pot lid on, she left them to stew for another three hours, before turning off the fire and waiting patiently for the liquid to cool. The process took her nearly a good day's work before she discovered, to her delight, that the dresses had taken on the color of the sky.

In a thrilled voice she beckoned her daughters to come over. An impetuous girl, Ah-Shui grabbed the dress and put it on before her mother noticed, only to find her skin was stained blue. That reminded Ma Gu about one more thing she needed to do. She hung the dresses out in an airy place for three days before putting them in salt water. When they were dry again, her daughters' dresses were the only clothes in the town with this special color.

Temperamentally the two girls were like chalk and cheese. Ah-Shan folded her new dress neatly and put it away for important holidays, but her sister wore it immediately and showed off from door to door, angling for compliments, which she was used to and of which she never tired. When she was small, everyone had said with a smile that Ah-Shui was the prettiest girl they had ever seen. As an older teenager, she was walking on the street one day as a teacher from school came nearer. He stood gawking at her as she passed him, and then turned to follow her for quite a long time. Rubbing his eyes, he thought of a fairy tale he had read the previous night, and murmured to himself, "Is this girl human or an angel?"

The two pretty girls brought Ma Gu's simple and dull family to life. Every year when the river rose, she would stand by the window to tell them about the flood disaster that they suffered years before. It was one of their favorite stories.

Ma Gu and her young husband had been strangers to Wuluo, and they came from a place far away that had been struck by heavy floods that year. After the place had experienced flooding for more than two months, they woke one morning, only to find everything had gone wrong: the trees on the east side were found on the west, and the sun was seen rising from the wrong direction. The floods had caused a terrible landslide, by which half of a mountain slope was steadily moved overnight from the north side of the river to the south side. The trees, houses and lives on it remained intact, as if they were a serving of scrambled eggs, moved from the pan to the plate. They remembered that they had felt dizzy in their dreams.

As they were adapting themselves to the new orientation, another heavy rain began to pour down, and soon much of their roof was submerged in the floodwaters. The two of them were floating on a raft they had prepared, while those with no rafts had to escape in wooden basins or on door planks. They floated on the surface of the water for a long time and they didn't know when they lost consciousness. When they recovered, they found themselves lying on a beach. They heard a tune as they were about to sit up:

> I asked the singer how many tunes you know
> As many as the hairs on an ox, he said
> He sang for three years and a half
> Until he could only croak
> It was only the hairs on its ear.

They turned to each other, smiling. They were swollen all over and gasping for breath, but recovered their strength unexpectedly. "This is a great place because we have songs," he said.

"Yes it is and I love songs," she responded. With a desire to shout, she cleared her throat and opened her mouth without thought to finish the song they had heard:

> I know more tunes than you do
> A mouse gnawed its way into my rice bin
> The leaked grains outnumbered all your tunes.

She had yet to finish what she was singing, but he was suddenly startled. This was the first time he had heard her sing. He had never expected her to sing so well, nor did she. Just as the right foot follows the left in a stroll, she started to pick up the singing just as the tune had stopped. Remaining on the beach for a long time, they wondered over the changes they had experienced, as if they had been reborn.

"So, why don't we stay?" he suggested.

They learned that the place was called Wuluo as they went into town. They built a simple house on the bank of the river. Everyday the man collected logs from the river upstream with the help of his wooden raft, while the woman took care of her vegetables at the riverside. Later he was invited to work with his raft, using his skills to collect things in water, and then became one of the first employees when a new shipyard was opened. They moved to a new house, where their daughters were born. All that they had previously owned—a house, a five-year-old boy, a couple of farm animals, a cat and a dog—were nowhere to be found, just like the floodwater on which they floated, leaving the two of them alone.

They had thought to end their lives at that time when they first recovered. It was shameful for them to live on when everything, including their son, was lost, and yet they felt a sudden impulse to sing. But the heavy mist in the town not only scared them to death, it also deadened their pain. Like two rocks in the water, they were swept all the way down the river before they found themselves ashore. Now that some sand was collecting around the rocks and a few clumps of green grass were emerging, they gradually forgot what had happened to them.

It was during that period of time, Ma Gu recalled later, that she began to develop another magic power. When she was alone, eyes closed and concentrating on one thing, she would feel something drifting before her eyes. It was a suggestive sign sometimes and a distant sound at other times.

It began with the job of her husband. When he heard that a shipyard was to be built in the town, and that the head would be the man who often came to the river to wash himself, he told her it would be best for them if he could be hired. In the state-owned factory, he would be paid monthly and receive a pension when he retired, meaning they could live a life they had never expected. He did not mention this with any seriousness or consideration, but just blurted it out when he talked about the job, because officially he was not a local resident and he had no idea how long they would stay. She didn't take it seriously, either, but she began to picture the life he had talked about.

When lying in bed at night, she heard a tiny voice speaking to her, "Go and dab some soap on the rocks at the riverside! Go and dab some soap on the rocks at the riverside!"

It was a weak voice, but loud enough to drive away her feeling of drowsiness. "Who is it? What does it mean?" she thought to herself.

She didn't sleep well that night, turning and tossing in bed. When she woke up early in the morning, she remembered what the voice had told her to do. "It said to dab some soap on the rocks," she thought, "so I'll do it and see what happens." With a small cake of soap, she slipped out to the river.

Later as it was getting dark, that man went to the river to wash himself as he did everyday. As he bent to pour water over his back, he stepped on the rock with the soap, and the fall stunned him. Busy with the logs he collected, Ma Gu's husband stopped his work and dashed over to help as soon as he saw.

"Thank you so much. You saved me from drowning in the river," the man told her husband days later. When the injured man recovered, he became the head of the shipyard, and Ma Gu's husband was hired as one of the first employees to work in the factory.

His family moved into a dormitory there. For quite a long time, Ma Gu was too scared to step outside her house. When she saw she was not caught out for it, she finally ventured for a walk.

Another weird thing happened to her soon after, when she went to the house of a nearby neighbor to borrow some cooking oil at dinner time. There was an elderly man in the family who had been blind for years, and she stared at his eyes for a while. Lying in bed that night thinking about the eyes she had seen during the day, a lamp appeared before her own eyes. A pair of scissors then appeared, coming over to trim the wick, after which the room was lit much more brightly. Immediately she fell under a mysterious spell. She got up to search for a lamp she put aside years ago, lit it, and trimmed the wick in the way that the vision had suggested. She felt it cost all the energy she had. She was overtaken by a wave of fatigue and went to sleep with the scissors still in her hand.

Hearing unusual noises coming from the neighbor's house the next day, she went over to see what was happening, only to find that the blind man was now able to see. He was only too happy to repeat his story to anyone he met, "It was as if a wick were trimmed. I had a slight pain and I opened my eyes and I could see!" Ma Gu wasn't surprised. She knew she had now become a different woman, but she kept silent. She couldn't tell anyone about it. It was a secret from a god, and she would lose this psychic power if she ever told.

Behind their street, in the area farthest away from the river, were rows of new houses, in which lived all of the town's neatly dressed people with their private cars. On their balconies they grew a variety of flowers, among which women were often seen reading, chatting or knitting after work.

Passing by the buildings, Ma Gu often wondered why wild flowers looked so nice when they grew on a balcony. After pondering for quite a long time, she dug out varied wild flowers for herself and potted them in broken wash basins in her yard. These flowers were fragile and they did not blossom, but she loved the rich color of young green, for which she felt great tenderness. They would snap off at a joint when a careless walker touched them. Her daughters were among those careless walkers who broke her flowers now and then, and every time they did they were scolded.

They would challenge her, "Why these delicate flowers? Rhododendrons are much easier to grow. You simply leave them in the yard and they grow well, in the rainy season or when it is very dry." But she would be sneeringly dismissive of their suggestion. "Is it truly a flower if it is not delicate? Why is it grown then? It is prized for its tenderness, you know."

Later she had a new idea. Her daughters would marry into families in that area, to grow flowers on their balconies and read, chat and knit beside them in their fashionable nightgowns. They deserve that lifestyle, she thought. She had never commented on the appearance of her daughters, but she was well aware they were the most beautiful young women in the town. How could they live in simple wooden houses at the riverside, as she did?

Thinking about the magic power she had, she decided to try it on her daughters. Many times she tried locking herself in a dark room with a red string in her hand, trying to picture her daughters as the wives of loving, rich men. But she received no hint. Finally she told herself that it could not be forced, and she just had to wait because it was a blessing from the gods.

Ah-Shui was hired in a tea factory after her graduation from high school at the age of seventeen, a time when young people sleep the sleep that knows no waking. Her mother bought a bedside alarm clock for her. But years later her mother would remind her, "You slept like a stone, and I had to come silence your clock every morning. Only when I literally dragged you out of bed, did you open your eyes. If I hadn't come to get you, you would have been late for work everyday."

Ah-Shui seemed to benefit from her beauty sleep. Every time after she woke from a long, peaceful slumber, her mother was surprised to realize how much more beautiful she was than before. With her pink-white skin, she looked as attractive as a perfectly ripe peach. She was dark-eyed with jet-black eyebrows. Her full lips were naturally pink, leaving people to wonder how firm they might be. When she smiled, her brilliant white teeth glowed.

With the natural sense of superiority that all beautiful women have, she had never been domesticated. Nor did she have the time. When she managed to crawl out of bed, it was almost time for work, so she had to snatch her keys to dash out the door. When she returned, food was already on the table waiting for her, but she would collapse into her chair looking too tired and drawn to eat, as if she had worked as a porter on a busy dock rather than a quality inspector in a tea factory. Tasks like doing laundry seemed to have nothing to do with her, as she had to stay away from soap and washing powder because she was allergic to all detergents.

Compared with Ah-Shui, Ah-Shan was something of household savant. Needing no alarm clock to wake her up in the morning, it seemed that her fate was mysteriously linked with the sun. She would rise at the crack of dawn, when it was still dark in the house and everyone else was in a deep sleep. The first thing she did, after she washed her face, was to clean every inch of the house, without making any noise to disturb the others. Then she lit the briquette stove and put on a pan of water. It was so well timed that the water would be warm enough for the other women to wash their faces just as they got up from bed. At the same time, she was already rubbing the family's clothes on a washboard.

Sometimes the last snores echoing in the house in the morning would upset her, and she would put Ah-Shui's clothes aside, intending to leave them to wash for herself. When the other clothes were all done, she would shake the soap suds off her hands while thinking about what to do with Ah-Shui's laundry, and ended up putting it into a basin and starting to wash.

"You're older. And older sisters are born to take care of the younger ones," Ma Gu said. She then turned to dress Ah-Shui down.

"Lazybones, the only thing you do is to sleep. Look at your sister. She's always ready with her hands."

"That doesn't mean anything. You know, I earn more money," Ah-Shui challenged her mother with a toss of her head. That was true. Ah-Shan worked as a ticket seller at the bathhouse in the shipyard. While people lined up at the gate during winter, the bath was almost empty in summer as the riverside filled with people with soap and towels in their hands. How much could money she make?

The two sisters were two years apart and looked like each other, but their temperaments were distinctively different. Besides doing housework, Ah-Shan would often sit in a movie theater to watch a film numerous times, until she was able to remember the lines of each character. Ah-Shui, on the other hand, when she was not at work had nothing to do but dress herself. She saved up for a hair-curler and used it regularly to style her bangs. When she overdid it, the house was filled with the smell of burning hair. At the end of her long plaits, she sometimes tied colorful strings and sometimes handkerchiefs, making it seem as if there were two butterflies fluttering around her waist.

Ma Gu sometimes stood staring at her daughters, wondering why one of them flittered around like a colorful butterfly while the other was as quiet as a gray moth. With their similar size and appearance, they looked like twins, but why weren't they alike?

No matter whether they were butterflies or moths, they were a major headache for their mother as they were reaching the age of marriage. They both refused any matchmaker's proposal, one of the few areas of agreement between them in all their years.

They said that they wouldn't be forced to go on a blind date, because what was meant to happen would happen on its own. Ah-Shui was especially upset when a matchmaker was mentioned to her, striking the dining table with her chopsticks and screaming, "Who are those old gossips? They are nothing compared me, but they are trying to find a man for me. What man do you think they can recommend? If they think the man is a good man, why don't they go and marry him? Leave me alone."

Ah-Shan declared even more boldly, "I don't think I can find my future husband in this town!"

Before long a new hairdresser opened a shop in the town. It was named "Old Shanghai," and the owner was a slight young man, a stranger to the town. People returning from the shop said it was the most luxurious hair salon in town, furnished with glass all round. It was so shiny that they claimed they were dazzled and couldn't even find their way back home. Others said the young man was the most handsome guy they had ever met, as strikingly good-looking as Ah-Shui in the tea factory. Hearing the comparison, Ah-Shui sneered and decided she would never visit the hairdresser. As the acknowledged premier beauty in the town for years, she was instinctively annoyed when anyone was admired more than she.

The hairdresser had grown to become a main topic of conversation among the locals. What the young man wore always came as a complete surprise to them. They couldn't understand why his coat was so short that it showed his naked waist, why he wore so many metal buttons and chains on his clothes, how he put on those weird pants with the incredibly thin legs, which looked like bandages wrapped firmly around his legs. His shoes were also strangely thick and so heavy that he could kick a pig to death.

The young man became a challenge to the traditional aesthetics of the town. The local people came to realize that, unlike themselves, he wore clothes not to cover his body but to highlight its features: his small, firm and sexy hips; his muscular thighs; the prominent bulge between his legs. They ached dully as they wondered what the world beyond the hill was like. A coat was no longer a coat as they knew it; neither were pants and shoes. And a man was different. The owner of the shop even wore a long ponytail, which left them speechless, standing with their mouth wide open.

The young man went even further. Every few months he would leave the shop in the hands of his assistants and go back to his own hometown, Haishi, a place whose name he pronounced rather strangely, and of which the Wuluo locals had never heard before. He would come back with clothes that not only had they never seen before, but were also beyond their very imagination. He was never seen in any outfit available in the local market, and he said he could not get used to those clothes. As they saw it, it meant he still had a long way to go in acclimatizing himself to the new place. Though a stranger, he ate the local food and drank the water, yet he refused the local way of dressing. As he had more clothes than he could possibly wear, a few bold young customers came up with the idea of buying some from him. He was finally persuaded. Sometimes he had to sell clothes he had worn only a couple of times, when they liked them so much that they insisted.

More and more young men and women visited Old Shanghai, and they were proud to be friends with the shop owner. Of course those who were not bold enough only stood on the opposite side of the street, looking. With his hairstyle, what he wore, what he looked like, and the shining tools he used in his shop, the owner was formidable to them. They would be too nervous to speak when they ventured inside. Even if they did, there was little understanding because they spoke radically different dialects.

Having heard too much about the hair salon and its owner, Ah-Shui could no longer resist the temptation to look at Old Shanghai. She was increasingly upset, as the focus of conversations about beauty in the town had shifted from her to the hairdresser. Everything he did increased their excitement or anxiety: the clothes or accessories he wore, what he ate or drank, the jokes he told. At the same time, she felt slighted. She hated the exaggerated tone they used. Those words, which had belonged to her alone for all the years before he arrived, were now used to flatter a man. Was it fair? Did anyone believe a man could be as attractive as a woman? She could never believe it.

One day she held a pair of tailor's scissors in her hand after she washed her hair, ready to trim the bangs hanging on her forehead, but she stopped. A sudden feeling of hatred toward the implement overwhelmed her. She dropped the scissors and, on her high heels, headed straight to the salon.

The young man was blow-drying a customer's hair when she pushed the door open. The hand holding the hairdryer shook a little as he noticed her, and she suddenly felt faint, holding the back of a chair to steady herself. Before her was a man she had never expected to meet. He had fair skin and chiseled features. Her heart skipped a beat when her eyes met his, eyes in which she saw something she had never seen in anyone before. It was beyond her description, leaving her almost gasping aloud in surprise.

When he smiled at her, she saw something brilliant flash over his face and felt faint again. Managing to remain calm, she moved a few steps forward and greeted him in the local language. Strangely enough, he understood her perfectly, just as she knew what he was saying in his distinct southern accent, which she had never heard before. Surprised at this first vital communication, the people in the town concluded beauty was a common language that went beyond barriers of dialect or accent. Because physically attractive people click immediately, the two of them talked to each other as they if were old friends, while the other locals had failed in understanding him even with the help of gestures.

The feeling of intimacy they shared was no different than that between two long-lost friends who meet in a foreign land. Leaving the customer whose hair was still to be dried, he started to think about how to do hers. With her long hair in his hand, he suggested a perm for a long curly style, after some trimming.

Hearing this she began to playfully shout at him, as if she were speaking to a lifelong friend, "Do you know what you're talking about? I have to go to work, you know. What will my superiors think of me if I have a perm? I have worked in the tea factory for less than two years, and I want to be promoted for my performance."

She realized she was not only exaggerating but talking too much to a stranger, and in an unexpectedly friendly manner. But she could hardly control herself and continued, unaware of what she was saying.

Staring at her while she talked, he kept smiling as he started braiding her hair. As he worked, Ah-Shui watched in the mirror the two fair moving hands of his, which looked like two butterflies on her head fluttering around each other in the mating season. He fixed his eyes on her face in the mirror. When they withdrew their eyes from each other in embarrassment, Ah-Shui found herself a different woman. But all he had done to transform her was to part her hair in a different way, and put aside her clips and rubber bands. She was surprised at his skills in making a woman look good, skills that many women had yet to learn themselves.

"How come I've never thought of these practical ideas?" she thought.

Ah-Shui became a regular visitor to the shop after that. He charged two yuan to trim a woman's bangs, but for reasons she could never explain, she handed him half the amount.

"I don't charge you," he said with a smile.

Old Shanghai became Ah-Shui's dressing-room. She rose every morning as the day was just beginning to break. As the door squeaked open, she would fumble her way in a frantic hurry through the thick mist, holding her black hair in her hand. While her neighbors were just waking from a deep sleep, they would hear her running footsteps along the street to the hairdresser's, and then the noise of her fist on his door. She was trying to wake him up as quickly as possible for her plaits.

"Why don't you stay here overnight? It would save you time on the way," he said with a yawn.

She didn't react to whatever meaning lay behind his words, looking at herself with rapt attention in the mirror. She wondered if she was really as beautiful as her image in the mirror, but she liked how she looked in it. She watched him in the mirror, as he lazily came down the steps and carelessly stood behind her with his legs apart. She jokingly called him "Haishi Man." She felt it was a close contest between them, and she would lose if she was not careful enough with what she wore and her appearance. As a true townswoman, she could not bear being beaten by a stranger.

In time Ah-Shui found herself in Old Shanghai nearly every minute she was not at work. She loved the large mirror in the shop. Examining herself and Haishi Man again and again from different angles in front of it, she came to see her own advantage. He was a man, but she was a woman. Handsome a man as he was, he admired women because he could not be interested in himself. She felt much relieved now. If Haishi Man admired any woman in Wuluo, she thought, it would be no one else but her. She was also sure that he was interested in women. She was happy when she thought she finally had the upper hand.

One day, as usual, she watched herself in the mirror when she was alone with Haishi Man, who was braiding her hair for her. Suddenly he stopped, lowering his head to kiss her on the cheek. It was so unexpected that she jumped up, holding her face in her hands and shouting at him, "What are you doing?"

"I love you. I mean it," he replied.

She stared at him for a while before she turned to run, going for quite a long time. Standing by the roadside, she found herself upset. What should she do? She ran out, so how could she go to his shop again? If she did, she would not be a good young woman. But who would braid her hair for her? He had done it for her ever since she met him. She knew well that he did it much better than she did.

For the entire next day, she fought off the impulse to go see him, trying to braid her hair herself, something she should easily finish in a minute. Strangely enough this time she tried her best, only to find it had ended up in anything but plaits. She then went to Ah-Shan, who was washing her clothes, for help. After quickly cleaning the soap off her dress, Ah-Shan took Ah-Shui's long hair rudely in her hands, as if it were bunch of wheat she was ready to reap. She began to twist it with string before pushing her away saying, "Done." Looking at herself in the mirror, she saw something resembling a cow's tail behind her head. She turned angrily and tried to kick her sister in the leg.

She was tense and restless for the whole day, asking whomever she met how she should have her hair done, "Is it better if I have my plaits cut off and get a perm?" She was impatiently told to go to Old Shanghai for a good idea.

It was late at night and she was standing in the misty street, thinking she would have to change her hairstyle if she wanted to be a good woman. She would no longer be "Miss Wuluo," an unofficial title she had enjoyed ever since Haishi Man became her stylist. It was hard for her to choose between being a "good woman" and being "Miss Wuluo."

She stood outside of the closed hair salon. Inside the owner slumped on a chair, looking no different than a drunkard or a slacker. Of all a sudden, he stood up, opened the door, turned off the light, and headed out. Ah-Shui followed him in the dark, hoping to find out where he was going. After a while she found herself on her way back home. When they were near her house, he stopped, looking up to the windows with light blue curtains. He then walked around in front of the building, raising his head from time to time, as if he was estimating the distance from the windows to the ground.

Haishi Man had finally made up his mind. He cleared his throat, murmured to himself and continued on. Was he going to her home?

He was going there. He was already on the second floor, ready to go upstairs. She lived on the top floor of the three-storied building. Yes, he was not going anywhere else but to her home. How could he do that? That was terrible—her mother would kick him out. She was busying herself arranging a blind date between Ah-Shui and the son of a director in a government department, a future husband she had chosen for her daughter from among quite a few candidates. Haishi Man would be asking for trouble if he visited her at this time.

Hearing a greeting from Ah-Shui on the second floor, her voice lowered to a whisper, he stopped before he knocked at the door. They came out to the street and were wreathed in a thick gray mist, disappearing from the sight of others.

"I'm going to your home to ask you to marry me," he said.

"Don't be silly! My mother won't agree. She doesn't want me to marry a guy like you. She doesn't like your ponytail. And she doesn't understand your accent," she answered.

"It depends on you. Do you accept?"

"But ... but she's my mom."

"It's you who will be with your husband for the rest of your life. Not her. Why does she get to decide?"

"Anyway she's my mother."

There was a moment's silence before he continued, "Ah-Shui, do you love Wuluo?"

"What can I do if I don't? You know I was born here," she said absently.

"Ah-Shui, go with me. Why don't we leave this place for somewhere else? I mean it."

She was surprised but with a forced composure she replied, "I can't. I have to work, you know, for a living."

"Why do you have to? If you leave, you know you won't have to work for a living," he said, kissing her again. This time it was not on the cheek but on the lips, his tongue into thrusting her mouth as quickly as it could.

She was stunned and her mind went totally blank. Unable to resist any longer, she had no idea what he was doing.

Chapter Three

As Ah-Shui was winning her game with Haishi Man, Ah-Shan met the man of her dreams.

She did indeed have a man of her dreams. The night she watched the Japanese film *Manhunt*, she had a dream in which the hero in the film came to her ticket office. He handed over 0.5 yuan, but when she reached out her hand for it, he withdrew his own, saying, "Aren't you Mayumi? Why are you sitting here selling tickets?" Mayumi was the heroine in the film. His words helped her understand that the ticket office should not be her workplace. Standing up she simply left with him.

She not only remembered the dream but reviewed it again and again. However she kept it a secret, and it would embarrass her as a young woman to talk about her dream of a man in front of others.

Several days later, she was burying her head in her work when she felt something strange. She raised her head and before her eyes was the scene from her dream, an exact copy of it. The hero from the film was in black and stood face to face with her. He fished for 0.5 yuan and handed it over, but when she reached her hand for it, he withdrew his own, saying with his eyes wide open, "Aren't you Mayumi? Why are you sitting here selling tickets?"

She stared in amazement and her jaw dropped, "Oh my God! It's just what happened in my dream."

Ever since, Ah-Shan had lived in her dream, unable to wake from it.

The hero was an engineer from the capital city of the province, who was invited to help the shipyard build a new, larger ship. With the name of Gao Binghui, he was addressed as Engineer Gao. Since he needed to wash daily, he visited the bathhouse everyday. When he was still a distance away from the ticket office, he would smile and shout, "Hi, Ah-Shan." His accent and his way of greeting were both unique, as the locals only greeted each other with either "Busy?" or "Eaten yet?" rather than the strange "Hi." The engineer used this greeting only with Ah-Shan, which left her feeling honored. Every time she heard the greeting, the sun glinting from his glasses, her heart pounded with excitement.

In the following days, Ah-Shan got up even earlier. She rose before the sun because she had to bake her spring roll, a delicacy filled with spices, vegetables, egg and a strip of deep fried dough. This was the lunch she made for Gao. Because noon was one of the busiest times at work for Ah-Shan, she was not able to go home for her midday meal, and she had to prepare it first thing in the morning to take with her.

One day when Gao saw her lunch, he pretended that his mouth was watering. She handed it over and he accepted without any hesitation, immediately biting off half of it. "You did it yourself? Great. It's wonderful," he flattered her.

She then promised to bring him a lunch box everyday. Actually her own lunch was much simpler and lighter, with cheaper ingredients such as shredded potatoes and kelp sprouts, but for Gao she included egg, deep fried dough and other nutritious things, making it tasty and hearty.

Since Gao so enjoyed the lunch, Ah-Shan tried to make it even better by including various fillings and spices, bringing him a spring roll with a different taste and color everyday. With his cheeks stuffed with food, Gao would give her a thumbs-up sign. "Ah-Shan, now I see you're the best spring roll master in the whole country."

His flattery made her all the more confident in trying new things. She experimented with everything she could think of, and all her dreams had something to do with spring rolls. One morning when she opened her eyes, she woke up her mother, blinking with sleep, and asked, "Where is my spring roll?"

Her mother looked into her daughter's thoughts and went to make inquiries about the engineer. "Ah-Shan, do you know what you're doing? The engineer is a married man," she told her daughter.

"I know he was, but they've split," her daughter said decisively. Ma Gu's face reddened with rage. Finally concluding she could do nothing but give in, after they had some bitter quarrels about it, she was told that Gao must have a woman back in the city because he went there for a couple of days whenever possible, and came back looking physically exhausted.

She hurried to her daughter and said, "Don't let yourself be cheated. He's a skilled engineer and he's handsome. He's simply not for someone in this small town. He must have his woman in the city."

Ah-Shan hated the topic of women in a small town, and she screamed at her mother, "What's wrong with a small town? Do you think people in a small town are inferior to those in the city? I know what you have in mind. You don't want me to leave; you want me to stay to do the housework. I don't owe you anything, do I? Even if I did, I've paid what I owed with all these years of hard work. Don't trouble me any more."

Ah-Shan knew she had gone too far. She remembered what Gao had told her, "It's simply unbelievable I met someone like you in this little town." She had mixed feelings about his words, but she decided to talk with him about it at some later time.

Ah-Shan didn't think much of her mother's ideas about "small town women." She recalled that dream of hers again and again, and she did not think it had come from nowhere. She could never explain why that dream she had after watching the Japanese film came true several days later. This led her to believe she was predestined to meet Gao, which meant she could do nothing about it and had no other choice but to accept it. She was so blinded by a strong feeling of happiness that she told herself, again and again, that because of the dream, she would face any difficulty and move on to wherever their relationship would lead her. She wouldn't care about what it was then or what it would be in the future. Of course she would not mention it in front her mother.

Ma Gu decided to confront Gao. After her addressing him as Mr. Gao, she started to tell him how dull, uneducated and obstinate Ah-Shan was, and complimented him on his excellent ship-making skills. She implied that her daughter was unworthy of him and she suggested he should leave her alone, trying not to cast a spell on her. She was still learning how to start again after failure.

She continued and continued. He stared at her aghast, unable to speak for a long time. Finally he understood her last sentence and held on to it, "I won't fail her. I will never do that."

The night she learned about Ma Gu's visit to the engineer, Ah-Shan responded with cold anger. For the first time at home, she was so seized with uncontrollable rage that she became like a cat with a burning tail. She smashed a couple of dishes and upset a washing basin, with pieces lying in shatters. She also slapped her sister in the face, because Ah-Shui was on her mother's side, saying that all divorced men played with a woman's affections. She then rushed out of the gate, leaving the broken pieces behind, and her mother and sister staring at each other in surprise.

Everyone in the family knew she went to the engineer. Without a word, she stood with her back towards him and sobbed uncontrollably, covering her mouth with her hand. Gao was smart enough to know what had happened without her explanation. He reached out his hand, hesitated for a while, and then put it on her shoulder.

"Don't cry. I'll have to do something about it," he said.

She turned toward him. She knew he would do something, and he was a man with ideas. She looked at him, waiting for a good plan, but he said, "We'll have to keep a low profile. We'll have to think more before we do something. You know what, we put ourselves in a difficult position when we made public displays of our affection for each other."

This was the first time he had talked about affection for her. He was not talking about love, but she was quite satisfied to hear it, because she thought a well-educated man of good sense would be judicious in expressing his love for a woman. At the same time she began to understand that Gao was right about her public displays of affection. Every morning she had been busy with his spring roll, allowing her no time to prepare breakfast and do laundry for the family. She rushed out as soon as his lunch was ready, leaving the cooker unwashed and the kitchen with a strong smell of spring roll. Her family would have been unhappy when they had to prepare their breakfast with their stomachs rumbling. This must have led them to hate her relationship and Gao himself. She realized something must be done about it.

Gao then switched to telling love stories about other people, but now he repeated the word "love" rather naturally. He said the highest level of love between a man and a woman was a feeling of empathy, a loyal and sincere relationship. It had nothing to do with living or eating together. What he said induced a total sense of inferiority in her, because her love for him was far from being at this level. She had no idea what empathy was, nor did she know what was on his mind when she was not with him. What she wanted was to be around him all day long, and all she could do was to cook his favorite food for him. She would be perfectly pleased when he was happy about her food, and when he wasn't, it would be one of the darkest of days.

The engineer continued, "But the highest level of love is the great love. It isn't for average people; it is beyond their reach."

Ah-Shan didn't quite understand what he meant. She asked what the sign would be.

The engineer said, "The great love is love buried deep in one's heart. It's part of you. For example, when a couple has a great love, they're one, not two. One gives up himself and becomes part of the other. At the same time, they live unnoticed in a crowd because they don't publicly declare their love for each other. It seems as though nothing has happened between them, and no one knows they are passionately in love. Everything clicks after they leave the place and everyone is surprised."

The engineer continued with sigh, "This great love isn't for regular people!" He looked deeply frustrated, as if what he treasured most was stored in a place he would never reach.

Ah-Shan was even sadder. "Your great love doesn't have other signs?" she asked. "Don't you think we need them? Do you think it is easy for one person to give up herself and live for someone she loves?"

At night Ah-Shan lay awake in her bed, unable to get to sleep. She loved him, but her love was all about being together day and night. She wanted her love to grow to the next level but she didn't know how to do it. Now she had to make a last effort to reach the great love to which he referred. She would live for him and he would be the love of her life. If he died one day, life would be meaningless to her. Thinking about what it would be like if he died young or had an accident, she would come close to tears. In the dark night, while the others in the family were all sound asleep in bed, she was making up her mind about her future with him. He would be the love of her life. She would never be happy with a different man. She would be whatever he wanted her to be. She would mould herself to fit his desire.

The first thing she did, as he had told her, was to try to calm herself down, acting as if nothing had happened. She needed to play it safe by keeping her head down. She got out of bed ever earlier, and when she prepared breakfast for the family, she filled a lunch box for Gao. After putting the box in a safe place, she started to do the day's laundry. No longer standing before his office with the lunch box in her hand, she left it for him, putting it through his window before everyone arrived for work. She regretted having delivered the lunch to his workplace in the past, feeling embarrassed and ashamed when all their colleagues knew what she was doing.

He smiled and made a face at her when he came to the bathhouse, no longer greeting her with a loud "Hi!" Without a word he returned the food box, taking it out of a plastic bag and putting it on her table while getting his bath ticket. He ate whatever she prepared for him. Sometimes the box was returned with small pieces of paper inside, with his words on them, or a movie ticket or key ring. Those were all small gifts, but every time, her heart jumped with joy. She had never talked about her favorite movies, but he knew what they were, which she explained as a mysterious understanding between them. She had an uncontrollable urge to smile and jump, and to tell whomever she met that she was a happy woman.

"Real happiness comes with empathy rather than being together day and night," she told herself.

Her mother finally discovered what Ah-Shan was doing. She didn't believe she could succeed in persuading her daughter to break up with Gao. As a woman herself, she knew women were always of two minds, hesitating when a choice must be made. There was little she could do if her daughter was madly in love with the man. Anyway it was her daughter, as an adult, who should make the decision. It would be a good marriage for her. What Ma Gu was not happy about regarding the relationship was the role her daughter played in it. Her philosophy of love was that the husband should love the wife more than she loved him. The wife would suffer if the husband was the dominant partner.

"Why do you have to bring lunch for him?" she asked. "He can go to the workers' dining room in the factory."

"What else can I do for him? Nothing."

"Are you joking? Why should you? He needs to do something for you."

"I do it for his love."

"You don't have to do anything for him if he loves you. I see, you're begging for his love. Stop it! You'll be a doormat in the rest of your life, if you don't."

"What do you know above love?"

Ah-Shan, who was hopelessly in love for the first time, gave up, thinking her mother knew too little about love to argue with her.

"She must never even have heard about great love," she thought.

Chapter Four

Soon the news spread amongst the townspeople that Ah-Shui at the tea factory, the prettiest woman in the town, was dating the Haishi Man at Old Shanghai. They were seen every night, walking hand in hand at the riverside in thick mist, as if they were a couple in a fairy tale. It was also said that they lived together, as she was spotted coming out of the hair salon early in the morning, neatly dressed.

Ma Gu asked about the rumor at the dinner table, but Ah-Shui easily swept away her doubts with an immediate answer while brandishing her chopsticks.

"What a bore! Do you believe I'm dating a hairdresser? He's a poor barber, in other words. If you think a barber is the only choice for me, you sell me short."

Ma Gu was rather pleased to hear her explanation. The quick-fire words lulled her into thinking the rumor was baseless. It would hurt to see her daughter with a rootless stranger whom they did not know very well. She had her own secret plan for her daughter's future, which was to marry Ah-Shui to the government official's son, who worked for a foreign trade company. If she succeeded, her daughter would be able to live in a house with a balcony that had pots of flowers. She had talked with a matchmaker, and they were negotiating a date for the two young people to meet.

At the same time, she had something more urgent to deal

with: the relationship between Ah-Shan and the young engineer.

For some time, she had been trying to find a matchmaker for Ah-Shan, to discourage her older daughter's interest in Gao. She knew well that the relationship between the two would not last. For one thing, she had no idea whether or not he had divorced his wife. It would be rude to ask him to show his certificate of divorce. To her, he didn't seem to be a self-disciplined single man. Another reason was that he would never be serious about his relationship with a local woman, as he was from the capital city and he would return there when his project was finished. Ma Gu had learned enough about the ways of the world to know that he would neither stay for the woman with whom he had an affair, nor would he take her away.

When it was dark, Ma Gu took out photos of the young men from whom she would choose Ah-Shan's future dates. She put them on the table one after another, in the way she played cards. Ah-Shan scanned the photos and asked with a sneer in her voice, "Why they look equally dumb?"

Hardly had Ah-Shan finished her words before a stinging slap across the face jolted her. With her head raised high, she gave a contemptuous little laugh and said slowly, enunciating each word clearly, "It's no use to slap my face. Nothing will make me change my mind. I love him and I'll marry no one else."

What she left unsaid was that they had been together. On that night he told the real meaning of great love, dedication, is a blend of body and soul, so they should give themselves to each other body and soul. This hadn't been the case with his ex, but he wanted to know if the two of them would make a beautiful couple. He kissed her while whispering in her ear, which helped her decide, on the spur of the moment, to give herself to him.

"Do you believe he's a reliable man? You know a reliable man doesn't divorce easily, right? Does a reliable man make a pass at an unmarried young woman?"

"He's not to blame for his divorce. It was his ex's fault; she wasn't faithful to him. He was hurt, you know."

"What a fool! You're fool enough to believe what he told you."

For the whole night, Ma Gu tried to persuade her daughter that it was not love but the feeling of loneliness a man felt in a new place that drew Gao to her. He would simply dump her in the end. With barely concealed impatience, Ah-Shan eventually sprang to her feet and bellowed, "I know well why you're against this relationship. Your unhappy marriage keeps you believing all men are devils. You're envious of our relationship. You had a broken marriage and live as a widow, and you hope I do just the same."

Ah-Shan started to run away as soon as she finished her words. Ma Gu snatched a knife and followed her daughter, shouting, "I'll kill you! I'll kill you with my knife!"

It was getting dark and a thick mist was coming down. Ah-Shan disappeared in the mist as soon as she was out of the gate. Ma Gu was running blindly when she felt a sharp prick on her feet, as if numerous needles were piercing her arches. She threw himself down, with the knife falling to the ground quite far away. She thought she had been electrocuted before she realized there was no broken power line around her. Nor could she see any needle in her feet. But the pain was getting so much worse that she could not help crying. She was absolutely terrified by the prick coming from nowhere.

The pain lasted for about a week and she stayed in her bed, shedding tears. She went to the hospital but it seemed the doctors could never agree about her illness, so she had to return home, trying to figure it out herself. Her first idea was that she should not have sworn she would kill her own daughter. And then she thought it was because Ah-Shan had touched her most sensitive spot, which provoked resentment.

She had her full share of misfortune, but she had also gone too far when she finally took her revenge. Her unhappy marriage had started when she was sold to her husband's family, and she suffered more than any other child bride. She still shivered at the thought of her experience having to sleep in a sheep's pen, eating grasses and wearing a straw cloak. Even when she was as old as thirty, she was still beaten by her mother-in-law, who had grown up as a child bride herself.

A devoted son, her husband was always on his mother's side and never came to help her, but at night he would demean himself by begging to sleep in her bed. When his mother died, and he had no one to back him up in the family, Ma Gu began to hold her head high, trying to regain what she had lost in the past. She did not keep herself busy all day long as before, and she was no longer a virtuous wife. She tried to ingratiate herself with her daughters, repeating to them her horrifying stories of being a child bride. Every time they listened, they would shoot their father a look of pure hatred, as if he was a formidable enemy. She picked on him, screamed at him, and railed at him, but he seldom reacted aggressively. Then she began to hit him. Every time she did it, she demanded shrilly, "Why are you a coward now? Did the death of that bitch leave you a bastard?"

She would kick him to the ground, sleeping on her large bed with her arms and legs stretched out. He would silently go to the bamboo bed in the corner, on which he had a dirty straw mat in summer and a shabby quilt in winter. What angered her was that he readily accepted whatever she did to him. He would go out every morning after waking, to go fishing with a couple of old men or to learn how to play chess. He didn't start conversations in the family, and the only thing he did was to read his chess books for hours.

One day, she hid some pieces of grass roots and stones in his rice, to provoke him into a conversation or a quarrel. When he finished the rice and saw what was under it, he was stunned for a moment, and then opened his mouth for the roots and stones. She grabbed his bowl from him, throwing it down on the floor before she started to sob uncontrollably. He remained indifferent, which drove her totally crazy. She didn't know what she could do to hurt him deeply enough so that he would beg her not to do it anymore. All she wanted was to see him beg on his hands and knees. That would be enough to remove all her bitterness if he did it only once. But it seemed he didn't care at all what was done to him, which resulted in more irrational and unreasonable treatment. In the end, she was not hurting him to give vent to her anger any longer, and she was reproaching herself for trying to hurt him.

But she never thought he would drown in the river. In the terrible flood they had experienced, many people were killed but the two of them survived. She distinctly remembered he said before his death that he was sorry his parents had not treated her well. Did he have a presentiment of what lay ahead for him? She missed him after his death. Actually she had never hated her husband himself; the hatred she felt was towards his mother. He had helped her instead of anyone else in the devastating flood, when he could have left alone. He never mentioned what he did during the flood when they quarreled, as if he had forgotten all about it.

The pain in her feet, along with her tears, disappeared on the seventh day, and Ma Gu decided she had to change. She would no longer be so critical of her daughter. Looking at her silent daughter for a long time, she said to her in a soft voice, "All I want is that the man you love loves you."

"He loves me. I knew it from the very start."

"How do you know? Tell me about it."

"It's not something I can explain, but I can feel it. I really do. Don't worry."

Ma Gu asked with sigh, "But why do I feel differently?"

"You should feel different. You can't feel it because he loves me, not you."

As soon as she finished, Ah-Shan realized she had said the wrong thing and slid out of the room with her head lowered.

Soon something else unexpected took her mind off Ah-Shan and Gao. Years later she said she finally understood why baby boys were always preferred, because a baby girl in a family meant you could never let your guard down for the rest of your life. You had to be ready everyday for the troubles she would make, not knowing what you were doing.

She shrugged and spread her hands, saying, "I have two of them, and they're only two years apart. It means my troubles may be doubled."

What happened with Ah-Shui was a blow still more bitter. For a long time she had had high hopes for her daughter, who was bright, quick and well favored. Many times she had pictured her future, believing her young daughter would bring a great change in her life. But her dreams turned sour, so quickly and helplessly.

That day, people noticed Old Shanghai wasn't open for business even when the sun had climbed high in the sky. They waited until afternoon but it was still closed. Strangely enough, Ah-Shui disappeared too; she was not at work. They pushed the door of the salon open and saw a scene of confusion where all articles of value were gone. Ah-Shui's room was clean and tidy, but a leather handbag was missing. It was a gift from the hairdresser. A stylish, name-brand bag, it was the only one of its kind in town, and she valued it more than anything else in her life.

Ah-Shui had run off with the hairdresser! Ma Gu locked herself in the house, shedding silent tears, muttering and swearing, and refusing to eat, until she was utterly exhausted. She thought about Ah-Shui day and night. She went out several times a day to see if the postman was coming in her direction with a letter from her daughter, but always in vain. It seemed as if Ah-Shui had forgotten all about them. Ma Gu could do nothing but swear to herself that she would never think of her daughter again, just as she swore to forget about her past and the son who had died in the flood that brought them to the town. But this time it was useless, and tears brimmed in her eyes immediately after she had dried them. Was she happy with him? Was she suffering? She was pampered at home, and she had never even washed her own dishes or socks. She got a rash on her hands if she washed clothes. She was more delicate than a wildflower.

At the same time, the first ship built in the shipyard was launched. With the cheers of a large crowd, it started to leave the harbor after sounding its whistle for the first time. Ah-Shan's eyes also brimmed with tears, as if she had contributed to the new ship. A farewell party was held in honor of Gao, who was about to leave. Ah-Shan went to him but he said he was busy with the transition process, and he would talk to her in a while. She turned to walk away but he called her back.

"Remember durable love keeps, without being together day and night. Do you see the beacon? My heart is with you as long as the light is on. When it is turned off one day, I'm dying but my heart is still with you."

She spat on the ground twice to protect against the unlucky thing he said, before she waved him goodbye with a smiling face and went back home to wait for him to come.

It was getting dark but she was still waiting for him. "He must be at a party or he may be half drunk," she thought, but she believed he could come because he said he would. She had never had second thoughts about his honesty. Then she nodded off to sleep. It was the next morning when she woke up, and she was surprised that he was not with her. Or he maybe he came but left when he saw she was asleep? Without washing her face, she rushed out.

The small house he lived in was unlocked and virtually empty, without even a picture on the wall. He was gone. She was told that he left last night, in a car.

Ah-Shan stood for a while before she turned to hurry back. She did not go back home, instead walking along the streets in the town, back and forth, for a whole afternoon. People thought she was looking for something or someone before they noticed that something had gone wrong with her. She foamed at the mouth and answered to no one. She was so powerful that no one succeeded in stopping her from hurrying on.

It was Ma Gu who slapped her hard across the face, with the

support of a crowd that was now following her, before she started to cry tragically.

Ah-Shan was from that point always seen walking alone outside, looking dully ahead and never responding to anyone. It seemed as if she had become an anxious mute. Worried as she was, Ma Gu locked her daughter in the house. All she could do was to arrange blind dates for her daughter as soon as possible. This time Ah-Shan showed no sign of disagreement; she went to meet different men as if she were a mere puppet of the matchmakers. But things had changed. Now she was often rejected, just as before she had her choice of whom to meet. Those who met her were wondering: Why was she so quiet? She didn't answer questions. Why was she silent? Would she be this way all her life? They had no answer to these questions.

One day when they were going out for another blind date, Ah-Shan stopped before her mother and said calmly, "I guess I'm pregnant." She then pulled up her shirt to show her mother, who was shocked to see a round basketball belly.

Ma Gu took a step backwards, and she knew she would now be seen as a disgraced mother in the town.

Chapter Five

Little Yu had been pretty sensible ever since she was born. A sensible person was usually quiet. She was never seen crying after she came wriggling and wailing into the world with her first breath. It seemed she knew at the very start that she was not welcome, and every noise she made would be a cause of shame to the family and fill them with terror. Years later, she was devastated when a dog's vocal cords were removed so it would not be able to disturb its neighbors at night. She suspected her family must have thought about whether to remove her vocal cords.

She spent much of her childhood in her house because whenever she stepped outside she would be the main focus of attention, and soon a crowd of onlookers would form around her. Her grandmother had to lock her up in the house, away from the kindergarteners and other kids. When sunshine was needed, Ma Gu would carry her to a small yard surrounded by a fence with logs and blocks of coal. Inside with her were tiny round stones and wood blocks as well as broken bowls and spoons. She crawled about on hands and knees, playing alone. Her favorite game was playing house.

Little Yu was becoming weak and pale, and she was terrified at the sight of the sun or a stranger. One day a visitor, who often came to help Ma Gu, stopped by to change the screen windows in the house. He stared at the little girl inside her fence for a while, and then said with a smile, "What a charming girl! Come over and let me give you a hug."

Little Yu stood gaping at the man before she screamed her head off. She had no idea what he would do to her, because she had never seen a new face or heard a different human voice. She was scared by the arms reaching out for her. She gradually calmed down when Ah-Shan rushed over with a pinch of salt in her hand, the highest reward she could receive. When she played house, she treated fine soil as salt, but the salt in the kitchen was not to be wasted.

Seeing what was happening, Ma Gu went away to wipe her eyes. She now understood Little Yu was old enough to go to school. Children of her age in the neighborhood were all ready for schooling. She couldn't lock her up for the whole of her life. Even if she could, the fence would fail one day; it would be impossible for her to make it higher, as she had already made it higher as time passed by. An even higher fence would be a prison.

When the visitor left, Ma Gu tore down the fence and put away the items for playing house. She washed Little Yu's face, dressed her, and went out with her to the street. She could no longer hide her, and she had to pluck up courage to take her to see the outside world. To her surprise, the girl refused to move after a few steps outside the gate and was about to cry.

"I'm scared. I want to go back home. Back home."

Ma Gu looked helplessly at her granddaughter for while, and then lowered herself to gather the girl up in her arms. She tried to calm her down.

"Don't be scared, Little Yu. We'll go for some candies. And we'll go for some cookies."

With her arms firmly around her granny's neck, the girl was still screaming in fear. It seemed as if they were crossing a fast-flowing river instead of standing on a street.

Patting the girl gently on the back, Ma Gu started to hum a vague tune without knowing it. Little Yu stared at her granny with her eyes wide open, as if the voice was from somewhere else. Ma Gu felt acutely embarrassed under the girl's steady gaze.

Finally Little Yu entered school, and she turned out to be an unexpectedly smart student. In just two months' time, she progressed so rapidly in her schoolwork that all her classmates were left far behind, as if they had learned nothing in kindergarten. However she improved little in other activities: She never skipped and danced along. She never chattered excitedly to her friends. She never put her arm around the shoulder of anybody. She never flushed with excitement. She walked calmly and sat quietly. She was like a shadow, light and noiseless.

Her essay on the topic "My Family" caught her teacher's attention. This is what she wrote about her family:

> There are three people in my family: Mom, Granny and me. My Mom is Ah-Shan. Granny told me Mom attempted to kill herself twice. She jumped into a river when she knew she was pregnant with me but was saved. And she wanted to jump off a building with me when I was born. Granny said she was a fool. She said whatever mistake a person made, he shouldn't kill himself. It will make one mistake into two and make it impossible to correct it. Mom is much better now after the two experiences, Granny says, and she has forgotten all about it. Now Mom does many things every day. She helps Granny with the housework, knits for the store, and tells me stories before I go to sleep. All her stories are about my Dad. He's an engineer and he's building a very large ship in a shipyard far away. It will take him many years. He will come back to visit us when he finishes the ship and take us to his place. The three of us will never separate from one another. Granny doesn't like her stories. When Mom talks about Dad, Granny tells me to go

to bed. Every time she does, I'm sad. It's a sad
day without listening to Mom's stories. The
story is always the same story but it's better
than going to bed without a story.

The teacher took her aside to ask, "Little Yu, is what you
wrote in the essay a true story?"
She replied, "It is! Go and ask Mom and Granny about it."
Her teacher sighed before giving back the essay to her.
There was another story she wanted to include in her essay.
She was seized with a violent attack of dysentery when she was a
little girl, but her grandmother didn't call the doctor. When she
recovered, Ma Gu said to her, "Little Yu, you're incredibly lucky
to be alive. Adults die of dysentery. You were in the bathroom for
four days. We thought you were dead already, but you gradually
came to life when we were ready to bury you."
Strangely enough, ever since then, she had never suffered
from dysentery or other illnesses, which she thought was one of
her wonders. She was proud of it, because it was said that no other
children had ever survived dysentery without receiving treatment
for it. She didn't include this story in her essay because she knew
intuitively that her granny would be offended.
At the age of seven, Little Yu felt that her grandmother began
to like her. That day a sudden dizziness overpowered Ma Gu, and
she vomited violently. Ah-Shan went to bed after she cleaned
the house thoroughly. She looked numb and dull nowadays, and
was not especially attached to anybody. But Little Yu feared that
her granny would die when they were all fast asleep. She was
desperately afraid of dead people. Every time when someone in
the town died and Taoist rituals were held for a whole night,
the low religious chanting, accompanied by gongs and cymbals,
would travel across to her room, keeping her awake all night. She
would nestle against her mother out of fear, like a newborn kitten
clinging to its mother for safety.
With Ma Gu moaning loudly in pain before her eyes, she

thought her granny was definitely near to death. Ma Gu also cried, "I'm afraid I'm really dying. This will be my deathbed."

The little girl trembled with fright but she remained at the bedside. Every time her grandmother vomited, she handed her a cup of water to rinse out her mouth. She thought it was the vomit that was poisonous; when it was removed, the patient would live longer. She expected her granny could at least survive the night. When it was well past midnight, the girl was so tired that she fell asleep at her grandmother's feet.

Feeling much better the next morning, Ma Gu woke the girl up. She stared at her for a long time and then she fished out some coins from her pocket, saying, "My good girl, go and get a tea egg for yourself." Ma Gu was a different granny ever since.

Little Yu was comfortably ahead of her class in every subject, which was the only thing she was happy about at school. But it didn't last long, because the girl who was always second on every test encouraged the other students not to speak to Little Yu. She threatened that she would ignore anyone who didn't do what she said. Little Yu had no idea why the girl was so popular that the students in three different years, from the third to the fifth, began to cold-shoulder her. She didn't speak a word all day long except when answering the teachers in class.

To make it even worse, she felt scared when it was time for morning exercises, taking breaks between classes, going to the bathroom, and, most of all, leaving for home. She feared that they would goad her from behind, or line up with their hands on each other's shoulders, like a train, to charge and knock her over. She was told not to cry or report them to the teacher, which, they said, would bring brutal retaliation. For example, they would mess up her dress with blue ink, tear up her exercise-books and textbooks, stick a slip of paper with the word "bastard" on her back, or put worms in her hair without her knowledge.

Little Yu hoped she could become a friend of the Monkey King in her favorite story, who knew seventy-two transformations, and to learn how to be invisible. Then she could go wherever she wanted and no one could see her.

Later her schoolmates transferred their attention to Ah-Shui, who Little Yu had never met but knew was her aunt. They told one another in the classroom that Ah-Shui was a bad woman and ran off with a man. Little Yu's mommy was also a bad woman, and all women in her family were bad women.

Little Yu was helpless, and she guessed they were right when they said all women in her family were bad women. She was born illegitimate; her aunt eloped with a man; and, with her fair skin and modest build, her granny looked like a woman who loved ease and hated work, while other grannies in the neighborhood were as dark and thin as old tree roots or as fat and flabby as bags of flour.

She stayed seated in a room filled with rude noises, afraid to leave. She knew a rain of laughter would fall on her face as she passed. Or they would dash over to knock her down, tease her, or throw clods of soil at her. She expected the day's classes to go on and on, with one teacher coming in when another was about to leave.

The third period started, and she remained seated like a motionless gecko on a wall. She needed to pee badly because she had porridge for her breakfast. She was afraid to go, fearing they would charge over as a group to bully her. She didn't care about the pain it might cause but she couldn't bear the humiliation.

It was then afternoon naptime, after the fourth period, but still she didn't go to the toilet. She was bursting to pee but it seemed to her that each door of the classroom was guarded by her classmates, as if they knew well she needed to leave. Thinking she would feel better when she was asleep, or that she could slip outside when they were asleep, she nodded off over her desk.

A good shake woke her. My God, she had wet herself! The ground under her feet was damp and her trousers were soaked, and the air was filled with a foul smell. She was surrounded by her classmates, who covered their noses with their hands, grinning wickedly.

Little Yu was asked to go home. The teacher was the only person at school who had been nice to her, but now she contemptuously told her, "Go back for a change of clothes. How could someone as old as you still wet herself?"

The teacher had a chalk stick in one hand and covered her nose with the other. Little Yu felt like a pile of dog turds.

Little Yu thought of death for the first time in her life. Many times she had heard her grandmother murmur to herself, "Why do I have to live on? It's better for me to hang myself with a rope; with my death all my woes will end."

Every time her grandmother said this, she began to picture someone hanging from a rope. She was sure she knew how to do it herself. She tied one end of a rope to the mosquito net pole and the other end to her neck. She gave the rope a gentle pull, and the mosquito net fell down. She was so frustrated that she cried for help from her mother, who answered her instinctively but remained where she was. She then screamed at her, "Bad woman!" Her mother answered again but remained motionless.

It was early winter. Ma Gu came and quieted Little Yu, who had been crying for no reason. Then she went to the yard to loosen the soil in her flower pots. She blew her nose from time to time, when she suddenly remembered it was her birthday. Putting her gardening fork away, she started to cry.

"These little bitches have forgotten my birthday. They have no sense of duty to the family. They've left me alone."

She then picked up a bottle of liquor and a packet of peanuts herself, and cooked a couple of dishes to celebrate her birthday with Ah-Shan and Little Yu. The two adults drank quietly until Ah-Shan began to feel a little drunk, repeating words like, "Your father is a ship builder." Little Yu had long had doubts about her father and the ship. She suddenly felt so tired of her mother's babbling that she went to the balcony.

After a while, Ah-Shan staggered across the room towards

Little Yu and asked, "Why don't we go and see your dad?"

Her daughter asked casually without turning her head, "How?"

Ah-Shan was leaning on her stomach over the balcony balustrade, and jabbered with smiling face, "Go straight ahead and you'll see him." It seemed she had too much to drink.

Little Yu could never explain what she had been thinking that day, and why she did what she did. She turned her head suddenly and said, "I know you've been lying to me all these years. I have no dad. Why don't you ask him to come over if I do. Go ahead. Why don't you move?"

Ah-Shan was taken aback. Staring at her daughter, she moved her lips but was unable to speak a word. Little Yu continued to challenge her, "Go ahead right now. Why don't you move? Are you scared? I know you are, because the man is only yours in your dreams, and you've been dishonest."

Ah-Shan seized her daughter by the arm and began to shake her violently. "I'm not deceiving you. You have a dad; he's an engineer. Believe me and we'll go to him, okay?"

Little Yu nodded, and Ah-Shan started to climb up the balustrade. It was more than a meter high but she easily put one leg across it, sitting with one of her legs on either side. She then turned and signaled with her hand for Little Yu to follow her.

Ma Gu came charging towards her daughter calling her name, as Ah-Shan hung half over the edge of the balcony. Taking her by the arm, her mother pulled Ah-Shan up with all her might and called for help.

With the assistance of some neighbors, Ah-Shan was saved. She would have been dead if her mother were not quick enough, the neighbors said.

When Ah-Shan was asleep in bed, Ma Gu took Little Yu by the ear, dragged her to her mother's bedside, and made her kneel down on a washboard as a punishment. She was not to get to her feet before her mother woke up.

Little Yu had been scared stiff. She knelt motionless on the board with a dreamy look in her eyes until it was midnight. The board was already wet with her blood, but she didn't feel pain in her legs. What her grandmother had said was ringing in her ears, "You want to kill my daughter? I'll kill you before you kill her. I dare you to do it again."

Ma Gu came in after midnight and sighed deeply before pulling her granddaughter up to her feet. The sleeping Ah-Shan turned over in bed and her breathing sounded heavy in the drowsy silence.

Chapter Six

For some time Ma Gu had a shiny rice scoop made of aluminum hanging upside down beside her gate. She also cut a hole in the door big enough and kept it open even in harsh winter when the stiff winds, along with snowflakes or raindrops, roared through it.

Little Yu's fingers were stiff and swollen with the cold, looking like vacuum-packed sausages. Doing her homework on a stool after school, she raised her head from time to time to stare defiantly at Ma Gu.

"Where do you get off ruining the door? I'm frozen to the bone out here."

Ma Gu pretended not to hear her.

She also kept an extra pair of chopsticks at the table. When the others in the family were about to start eating, she would tap whomever was in front of her on the shoulder for the chopsticks. Then she would kneel down and move around under the table with them in her hand before putting them back on the table with an attitude of devotion. Little Yu knew her grandmother was up to her tricks again, but she was afraid to ask her about it. Ma Gu would never tell her the truth even if she asked. To similar questions, her answer was always, "Never ask a question you shouldn't ask."

The cat was finally let out of the bag one day, when Ma Gu murmured to herself, "Nine times nine makes eighty-one.

Eighty-one months have passed, and Ah-Shui is coming back. No one can cross this limit."

Ah-Shui did return home one night.

A power failure plunged the whole house into sudden darkness. Ah-Shan and Little Yu had to have their supper by candle light, while Ma Gu sat in the dark, listening to their crunching, swallowing her own saliva caused by the smell of the food. Everyone was surprised when the candle flickered and a figure appeared in the doorway.

"Mom," the figure called.

Ma Gu jumped up from her chair but she was silent, gazing at the figure as if it came out of a dream. After a minute, the figure reached a hand out for another's arm and a taller figure appeared before them.

"Mom, it's Ah-Shui, come back home. We're here to see you."

With their hands together, Ah-Shui walked toward her mother. "Mom, this is Huang. Do you recognize him? We're back to visit you." She pushed him slightly.

He called her "Mom" awkwardly, and Ma Gu answered, but rather vaguely. When Ah-Shui called her "Mom" again, in a sweet childish voice, she cleared her throat and said, pointing to a chair in the room, "Please sit down."

Seeing Ah-Shan coming over to her, Ah-Shui addressed her as sister and then patted her shoulder affectionately.

"You've gotten rather plump. What have you been eating when I wasn't at home?"

Ah-Shan smiled without speaking a word. The expression on her face was hard to interpret. She was smiling but it seemed she was reaching back into the past.

When her eyes fell on Little Yu, Ah-Shui looked the girl up and down for a while before turning to her mother, "Who's she?"

With Ah-Shui's hand in hers, Ma Gu went to the neighboring room. After a long while, Ah-Shui rushed out and held Ah-Shan in her arms, calling her name with a tearful voice. She then turned to pick Little Yu up, "Call me Aunt; I'm your aunt."

The first thing Ah-Shui's husband did the next morning was to visit his Old Shanghai. Looking at him from the back while peeling her vegetables on a stool, Ma Gu said to herself, "Everything has changed. There's no barber now; we call it a hairdressing salon."

She stopped for a while and then continued aloud, "He's much older, not as handsome as he was." Her tone of voice was rather flat, and no one knew why she was like this in the early morning.

It seemed she suddenly remembered something. With a threatening look on her face, she asked Ah-Shui, "Let me ask you. Where's his ponytail? And those wacky clothes? Now he dresses as we do, and I can't even recognize him."

"Why are you so short with him? I'll have you know, it was his suggestion that we come back to visit you. He said it was time for us to come back."

"What a generous man he is! But I've been doing quite well without you. You leave! Clear out of here! I don't want you back home," Ma Gu replied.

"Mom, Mom. What are you doing? You fly into such a rage, and it's not good for elderly people like you. You think I wasn't willing to come to see you? I thought you wouldn't be glad to see me. I regretted my decision the day I left, already when the car reached the slope of the hill. I wanted the car to stop but the driver wouldn't do it. He was angry at me because he might not have been able to start the car up again if he stopped. He wouldn't stop when we finally reached the top of the hill, either. The long, steep downhill slope behind us, you know, was so truly frightening. You know what, the car would have rolled down like a loose rock. I had nothing to do but leave with him."

Staring at Ah-Shui with her unblinking eyes, Ma Gu asked with sudden violence, "You think I'm easily fooled?"

Ah-Shui laughed while rubbing her hands on Ma Gu's chest, to help suppress her mother's anger. Ma Gu's tears brimmed over and fell on her cheek. It seemed as if they were brought about by Ah-Shui's movements.

Ah-Shui said, "Dry your tears. I'll cry if you continue. You'll be scared if I cry."

Ma Gu replied, "It's time for you to weep. I was in floods of tears every day after you left. I would have killed myself if I didn't have your sister to take care of. It seems I owe her a debt that I will never pay off."

"Mom, I'll stay this time. Wuluo is the best place for me. The weather is awful beyond the mountain, and the food is not as good as what you prepare. You can see, I'm dark and thin now. I was different before I left. I've been missing you all, you know."

Ma Gu reached her hand out to touch Ah-Shui's face. She slapped it gently and began to sob again.

"You're a lousy daughter. I raised you but you left without a word. And you didn't write me a single letter all these years."

Ah-Shui was sobbing, too, "I was afraid I would miss you day and night if I wrote. Mom, I won't leave any more. I'll stay with you in the town. Look what you have in the house. Ah-Shan is not healthy enough and Little Yu needs your help. You'll be quiet and alone without me."

"Do you know what you're saying? This is my family. You have your own. It's good that you came to see me, but you'll be laughed at if you stay here too long. But do they treat you well over there?"

"I'll tell you what, Mom—when I got there I learned he was a divorced man with a six-year-old son. The locals want to have more kids but they're not allowed to because of the one-child policy. They choose to divorce and then get remarried. Some of them divorce two or three wives and have several kids running around in the family."

Ma Gu kept silent, staring blankly for a long time at a bamboo basket directly outside. Ah-Shui stole several glances at her, rather guiltily. She had just risen to leave when Ma Gu said, "Then you've got to be nice to his son. This is what's predestined for you. You've got to accept it. No one can escape destiny."

Ah-Shui took her seat again to continue the conversation, "I got along well with the boy at first, but later I was somewhat tired of it and we're not that close now. They say a stepson is definitely different from having your own son."

"You're wrong. You've got to be nice to him forever. And you should never regret marrying the man. Even if you do, keep it a secret from me. I don't want to hear anything about it."

Ma Gu continued with a sigh, "No one is in control of his own destiny. Do you still remember that young man? I mean the son of the official. A matchmaker recommended you meet him. It's good you didn't meet. He got married after you left but soon he was in trouble. He had good job in a trading company, but he changed his mind, and joined a project to dig a tunnel. He said the road up and down the mountain was a barrier to the town's economy, so they started to build the tunnel through it. You know, so people could go in from this side of the mountain and come out from the other.

"He needed a large sum of money for the project, but the government didn't have it for him. He tried every means possible to borrow money from the banks, but in vain. To make it worse, a large quantity of sheepskins he had purchased rotted in his warehouse because they were not treated in time.

"The company suffered greatly and he got fired from his job. His father tried to smooth things over but he was not forgiven. Poor man, he was trying to take on these thankless tasks. You would have had a lot to cope with if you had married him. His wife worried herself sick about him."

"What did he do after that?"

"He managed a clothes shop at first. They said his father wasn't happy about his small, insignificant business. He went to the store to argue with his son and smashed a windowpane."

"Interesting man. Is he in the same business now? Where's his store?"

"He opened a restaurant not long ago, someone told me. A

hot-pot restaurant, I think. Well, what do you want? Why are you asking all these questions? Mind your own business! You have your own family but you really have nothing for yourself. The kid is not your own kid. It's been a long time since you left. Why don't you have one?"

Ah-Shui wanted to tell her mother that she had remained childless because she was thinking about divorcing her husband. She took one glance at her mother and the words stopped at her lips unsaid.

"So you're not living the happiest life in the world? You're one of those people who are too stubborn to spread their bets."

Upset again, Ma Gu tossed her vegetables aside and kicked a couple of green leaves away as hard as she could.

Ah-Shui felt she should change the subject. Seeing Ah-Shan doing laundry in the yard, she said, "I never expected to see Ah-Shan as she is now."

Immediately she realized this was another bad topic. Ma Gu said, as if with hatred, "Serves her right for being so stubborn. I wanted to argue with that engineer, but she stopped me by kneeling in front of me and threatening me with death. She told me not to make things difficult for him because he was already in a stressful situation. She told me to put myself in his place. You know what, she said he didn't trick her and she agreed to everything. You both got what you deserved, you and she."

Ma Gu blew her nose. "You have no idea how miserable I was in those days. My heart ached day and night. She was pregnant with Little Yu and was as sick as a dog; she vomited up whatever she ate until she was little more than skin and bones. She wept silently in bed every night. I was so furious that I did go to argue with him. Why wouldn't I? Sex involves two partners, yes, so how can the man escape when the woman is pregnant? I couldn't care less what a bigwig he was in his factory. Mercilessly I screamed at him for three days until the head of the factory came to see me, and he was suspended from his position. When

Ah-Shan heard the news, blood spat out of her mouth. And she became a different person."

Ah-Shui sighed, "My sister loved him. I have no idea why she was crazy about him. He was stout as a barrel and dark as a gypsy. What's more, he was heartless. He would've begged me to stay with him or I would've killed him, if I were Ah-Shan."

"Don't say that about Ah-Shan. What was the good of your Haishi Man? He was as thin as a rake and he had long fingernails and a ponytail like a woman."

Ah-Shui said with a snort, "You're wrong. Let me ask you, what good was my father? His face was set and hard. He was standoffish to you, as if you were his landlord. But you cooked whatever he liked for him and served him his share of food at the table for three years after his death. No one does it for three years now; three days are too long for them."

"I had to be different. We were husband and wife for life, for better for worse. I knew what I was doing even if I didn't like what he did. What about you? You young people have no idea what you're doing! You're arrogant and flighty."

After lunch Ah-Shui went out, along with her family, to buy clothes, food and other necessities. They also went to the photo studio to have a family photo taken. Ah-Shui had a handbag with her, and it seemed she had an endless pile of money in it. When she paid for something, she took a thick wad of notes out and casually pulled a couple of bills from it for the cashier. The whole town was startled by her shopping splurge. The shopkeepers who had gathered to kill time by playing cards hurried back to their empty stores, waiting for Ah-Shui and her family to come.

With her hand in Ah-Shui's, Ma Gu was dragged from shop to shop. She complained that Ah-Shui was flinging her money around, but her moaning stopped when they came out of the stores with heavy bags in their hands.

"Does he mind when you spend so much?" she asked her daughter.

"Why should he? The money is also mine. And it's time for me to buy my mother some gifts."

Ma Gu's face gradually relaxed. She had never picked up so many things on such a spree.

The most exciting moment came when a gathering crowd followed them to a jeweler's to take a closer look at the silver and gold items. Ah-Shui seated her mother on a bar stool, which allowed Ma Gu to examine closely whatever was in front of her eyes. Soon her mother had a ring on her finger, a shiny pair of heavy gold earrings in her ears, where not even the tiniest studs had been seen for years, and around her neck with its loose and wrinkled skin hung a cold, fine chain.

Ah-Shui moved a large mirror in front of her mother so she could see what she looked like wearing the jewelry, while she kept asking, "It's a nice piece of jewelry, isn't it?"

With all the gold before her, Ma Gu felt dazed, and had her mouth half open. For a time she wondered whether she should focus on herself in the mirror or on the shining gold things. Like rabbits in a small cage, her eyes leaped in utter bewilderment.

Ah-Shui then put a ring on Ah-Shan's finger and a little gold necklace around Little Yu's neck. The people around them clucked in disapproval and then dead silence followed. Turning her head Ah-Shui saw her mother sobbing quietly.

The four of them went out of the shop with their gold things, heading back home. Ma Gu continued to sob, drying her eyes from time to time.

"Mom, I know those are tears of happiness, but stop it! I'll pick up a couple of pieces for you every year, if you like."

The mother started to scold her, "You heartless daughter. Do you think I'm wild with excitement? I was thinking about your sister. She could've been a different woman if these things had never happened to her."

Ah-Shui suddenly realized that Ah-Shan had been quiet, fiddling with the ring with her head lowered. Ma Gu said in a whisper, "Do you think she can wear it? She will just lose it."

"What does it matter if she loses it? She's a woman and she should know what's like to have a ring on her finger. Tell you what, Mom, we've got to marry her off."

Ma Gu started to weep, "I'm afraid she's getting left on the shelf."

Ah-Shui was thinking about how to reply to her mother when she saw a man standing right before them, blocking their way.

The man started to walk towards Ah-Shui and then said, "Hello, I'm Qin Ziqing. You may not recognize me any more but I know who you are."

Ma Gu's eyebrows rose in great surprise. She realized it was the man she had arranged for Ah-Shui to meet on a blind date, before she ran off with Haishi Man.

The other three women left for home, leaving Ah-Shui and Qin Ziqing alone.

Chapter Seven

Haishi Man had to go back home for business, but Ah-Shui told him she had to stay longer for her sister's marriage.

Coming back from the bus station, Ah-Shui said airily to her mother, "If I get divorced ... why are you looking at me that way? To get divorced isn't shameful. It requires courage, you know. A coward never walks out on someone."

Ma Gu's mouth dropped open in surprise, and after calming down, she said in a weak voice, "What should I say when people ask me about it? What a shame it is to me! You were head over heels in love. What's wrong with you two now?"

"It's me. I didn't see it but now I can tell it's a problem. You tell me, Mom, is someone worth loving if he is only a hairdresser? Nothing else in life but cutting hair!"

Ma Gu jumped to her feet. "That's your excuse for a divorce? You've gone crazy. A hairdresser makes money to support the family. What else do you expect?"

"Mom, that's not what you said about my father. You said he thought of the sea when he saw a river, and he wanted to build a ship when he saw a raft. You said he was the most able man you'd ever met. He was worth all the men in your village, you told us."

What Ah-Shui said was true, so Ma Gu no longer argued. Her husband hardly cared about whether they had better food or clothes than others. He never thought about those sorts of things. What mattered to him was if his ideas were better, or whose designs were more appealing than his. He seldom spoke, sometimes remaining silent for days. No one knew what he was thinking about. He ate, walked, worked and slept as an ordinary person, but only those who understood him knew that he did all those things as a sleepwalker, without thought. Once in a while he would speak suddenly, but no one could understand what he meant. When he was asked, occasionally he would give them a word-for-word transcript of what had been said but usually he would ignore it. It seemed he hated to repeat himself. His words were like an early morning mist, which vanished without a trace.

One day he picked up a shell-shaped rock and came to the conclusion that Wuluo had been part of a boundless sea many years before. No one believed him; they didn't seriously consider his theory. They believed what happened many years ago had nothing to do with them, and they didn't trouble themselves with it. What they cared about was what they would have for their next dinner, or whether it would be sunny or rainy the next morning. He was in a permanent daydream, they all agreed.

Ma Gu wished she could stop him from his daydreaming, imaging that she could split open his skull to clean his brain with a sponge. She believed his brain had become clogged up with something, which she could wash away to bring him back to a normal life. But on second thought, she was afraid her life would be too dull without the anger and the many questions and troubles that came along with his daydreaming.

They had lived in a small village in the remote mountains before they arrived at Wuluo. For a time he stared dreamily at the village's one-meter wide stream, which wound its way through the hills. He believed the waters in the world were connected. No one else knew that the earth was mostly covered with water, with only a few land areas sticking out of the vast expanse. He spent a couple of months deciding that he would build a boat, with which he would follow the stream all the way down to the sea. He started to work at once by collecting the strongest vines and boxwood in the forest. Then he went to the blacksmith's shop for the longest iron nails. The journey would be long and tortuous, and there would be unpredictable dangers in the raging torrents waiting for him, so the only thing he could do now was to make his boat virtually indestructible.

Many neighbors came to see what he was doing, and they laughed at him. They had never seen a boat all their life, because what they had in the mountains were only a couple of little bubbling streams. They didn't even need bridges. They could step over a stream in the dry season, and a log would help them to cross in the rainy season. They thought it was a crazy idea to build a boat, jeering at his fancy.

He had finished the bottom part of his boat just when the most devastating flood in history struck the village from a nearby valley. The villagers managed to survive but were in a living nightmare, stuck in their waterlogged houses filled with the overpowering smells of fish and the rotten bodies of farm animals. They screamed at him for his boat, which they believed was the cause of the flood. Ignoring the neighbors, he stood beside the stream, staring at the rising water. He was pleased at the thought that the flood was caused to prove his theory. But he feared his boat was too small for the many villagers, and it was hard to decide who was to go with him in it.

He was still struggling with the decision when another flood hit the area as everyone was asleep, which left the whole village in the water and everyone writhing for breath. It was completely dark and he couldn't even see his own hand. It was impossible for him to choose whom to save, so he got hold of a person directly in his way. The two of them struggled in water like two drowning cats, climbing onto his unfinished boat when they were physically exhausted. When he realized it was his wife with him in the boat, he was completely amazed at how their marriage was predestined. Hearing Ma Gu screaming hysterically for help, he realized his five-year-old son had been swept away. They lost consciousness, from the pain of losing their son and the injuries from the giant waves and hidden rocks. They found themselves in Wuluo when they came to their senses.

If he hadn't hit upon the wild idea to build a boat, the two of them would been taken away, along with other villagers, by the floodwaters before they realized what was happening.

Of course he had been treated with scorn and ridicule in the family during the days the boat was being built, for the time cost him a season of potatoes, three *mu* (1 *mu* is about 666.67 square meters) of corn. and more than a dozen goats. He had been absent-minded ever since he started to consider the question of how much water covered the earth surface.

Ma Gu then stopped herself recalling the past and what her husband had done. She said aloud, "He was no ordinary guy." He would go ahead whenever he had an idea and never failed. He wanted to a build a ship and even the heavens helped him with a massive flood.

With her arm around her mother's neck, Ah-Shui said in a silky persuasive voice, "Mom, I'm just like you. Neither of us likes guys who can't see beyond their noses. We love men with vision."

"What's the use of vision? Those men are like kids, and kids drive you crazy."

"That's why we love childish guys."

Chapter Eight

Ma Gu started a home renovation project. She hung a small round mirror centered right above her gate, tied a bundle of mugwort on each door, and placed several peach branches on her bedside table. She never forgot to burn three sticks of incense in her kitchen before going to bed, even when she had a busy day and had to work late into the night.

She said, "I told my damn hubby the house had bad feng shui, but he simply didn't listen to me." Ma Gu was sure that something was wrong with the house, and that her additions of a round mirror, mugwort and peach branches would help to improve its feng shui.

At the same time, Ah-Shui started her program to make her sister, Ah-Shan, into a different woman. She cut Ah-Shan's tousled hair into a sleek pageboy style, and then removed Ah-Shan's clothes and had her put on her own dress and shoes. From behind it seemed that Ah-Shan was miraculously transformed, although she still had a vacant look on her face. She appeared normal as long as she remained silent.

Ah-Shui said, "We won't try to find a husband for my sister in town. It will be easier in the poorest countryside. I've been traveling these years and I know everyone wants a shortcut to city life. A guy like that will probably come to us. This is what we want, isn't it?"

She continued, "Ah-Shan loves Gao Binghui, doesn't she?

The best cure for her problem is to find a Gao Binghui for her. I should've thought of it years ago."

Sometime later an eloquent woman from the countryside came to visit, bringing along a plain-looking young man. It so happened that the man had the surname of Gao.

Ah-Shan looked at him with no expression before she focused on her knitting, not raising her head again. It would have been an embarrassing situation if the woman had not been talking the whole time. She listed what Ah-Shan had, as if she were checking out the goods in a store, "This is an apartment with two rooms and one setting room. It has an area of eighty-five square meters, and Ah-Shan's room is about eighteen with a set of furniture." Gao checked his urge to look around the house, remaining seated rubbing his hands.

Ah-Shui then added, "All these belong to Ah-Shan. I live somewhere else. I'll move out."

Ah-Shui gave the matchmaker a meaningful look, and the woman continued, "And they have rented a house on the riverside street. Why don't the two of you run a snack bar? Ma Gu is an amazingly good cook and Ah-Shan is also good at cooking."

When they came back from the riverside house, Gao changed his clothes to a white shirt, blue pants and spectacles with plain glass. He looked so uncomfortable, either standing with his hands at his sides or walking in an uneasy manner. Bringing the man towards her sister, Ah-Shui said, "Ah-Shan, he really looks really Engineer Gao. I mean it."

Hearing the word "engineer," Ah-Shan left her knitting aside and rose to walk around the man before she said aloud, "This man is a little like the engineer, but the engineer has better style and is as handsome as a movie star."

The man was acutely embarrassed and his face turned lobster red. It was just then that Ma Gu told them their lunch was ready. While the others went to see the riverside house, she had conjured up a superb meal. Having to keep adjusting his glasses, Gao asked Ah-Shui if he could take them off. She refused, suggesting he would have to get used to them. He then asked, "And the white shirt and blue pants?"

"I guess you have to at first, but you may change clothes when Ah-Shan accepts you," Ah-Shui replied.

A couple of days later, Gao returned with several bunches of dried day lily and cowpea flowers in his bag. He stood outside the gate, looking awkward. Ah-Shui took his bag, pulled him inside, and told him to change into the clothes she had prepared for him. Looking in the direction she pointed, he saw two sets of clothes, one white and the other blue. Feeling a surge of embarrassment, he noted it wasn't easy to keep white shirts clean.

"You don't do the laundry; it's Ah-Shan's job," Ah-Shui said.

"But you need bars of soap," he answered.

She waved her hand before her face, laughing. "Bars of soap? They're nothing. Don't say that again otherwise they'll laugh at you when they hear it." Gao was even more embarrassed and never mentioned it again.

At night a noise was heard from Ah-Shan's room, and immediately she opened the door and rushed out, her hair loose. She got hold of Ah-Shui by the arm, screaming, "Come on! Get the man out of my room. He's in my bed. Who is he and why is he sleeping in my bed?"

Letting out her breath in a sigh, Ma Gu picked up a torch she had placed beside the door and put a match to it. The mother moved the burning torch up and down before her daughter for a while, which gradually calmed Ah-Shan down. She went to her room with unsteady steps, yawning hugely.

"What's that smell?" Ah-Shui asked between sniffs.

Ma Gu clapped her hands, "Don't be so damned smug about it. I am the one who put the finishing touch to the plan."

All of a sudden, sleep overtook Ah-Shui and she put her teacup aside. She went to bed without brushing her teeth, trying to conceal her yawn behind her hand.

It was a good night's sleep for the family.

Ah-Shan and Gao's snack bar was finally open for business.

Ah-Shui named it Gaoshan, telling everyone that the two words were from their names, and the snack bar needed to be treated as their baby.

Gao lowered his head to think about it before he asked, "Will we have our own baby?"

After an initial surprise, Ah-Shui said, "It all depends on you two. You'll have one when you want to have one. Right?"

They only served breakfast when the snack bar first opened. It became a place where Ma Gu gave a flamboyant display of her cooking skill. She busied herself creating one bowl of delicacies after another. Visitors flooded in and wolfed down what they ordered before her eyes. Mopping the sweat from her brow during a break, she was absolutely satisfied with what was happening. Everyone was greedily shoveling in the food, nibbling away at that limited pile of grains measured for them before birth, while her own pile stood high. Her stomach was rumbling and her mouth was watering, but her face was glowing with satisfaction and happiness.

Her dishes made from flour were lovely and moist, and her pickles and kimchi left a delicious lasting aftertaste. Her noodles with yellow beans, already a classic dish in the area, were immensely popular with her customers, many of whom traveled all the way down from the surrounding villages to devour them, sweat glistening on their foreheads. They usually left with takeaway for their families. At the same time she put a wok on one side of her cooker for Ah-Shan, and taught her how to cook glutinous rice cakes, spring rolls and kebabs. Ah-Shan was excellent at making spring rolls, and in a few days' time, the line of people in front of her was just as long as her mother's.

More and more people came to Gaoshan, believing Ah-Shan's fried foods and kebabs were in a class of their own while her mother's noodles also tasted delicious. They believed that Ah-Shan, who was a bit brainless in their eyes, would never cut corners; she always served the amount she promised and didn't add any artificial flavor enhancers. Mentally deficient people played no tricks, they believed. When paid for their food, they preferred a handicapped businesswoman to a profiteer. It seemed they agreed that to choose Ah-Shan's food was to support charity.

Ma Gu felt awkward when a customer refused to order her noodles after the spring rolls sold out. She realized for first time that the customers came for Ah-Shan, now the head chef, rather than her own noodles. Switching from her own dishes to Ah-Shan's spring rolls that afternoon, she understood how distinctive the taste was, and how the seemingly absent-minded Ah-Shan was the better chef. Thinking about how Ah-Shan had prepared lunches for Engineer Gao, Ma Gu knew her daughter had often wasted food, putting a spring roll aside when she was not happy about its taste and starting to make a new one, until she had the best one for the engineer's lunch box. She would rush out of the door with it, leaving the leftovers on the kitchen table. Sometimes what she left behind was enough to feed the whole family for a day.

Gao had never expected they would do so well. Every day when the last customer left, he would open the shoe box, which they used as their till, and count out the money they had earned. Many times his hands shivered slightly because he had never possessed so much money. During the first days, he kept wondering if the money was actually their own money, or if he would earn that much every day.

Last month, before he came to town, he had lived in an adobe house, staring at the dirty roof and wondering where he could get the money to buy himself a new tube of toothpaste. He then remembered what a traveling blind fortune-teller told him, "You'll be rich or powerful at the age of thirty." He was amazed at how accurate the blind man's prediction was—he was thirty now, he was much richer, and he was the head of his family.

While he was thinking about himself, he could not help stealing a sidelong glance at Ah-Shan, who was rather a beauty when she was not talking. Ah-Shan was a hard-working woman and so many people were crazy about her food, even while more than a dozen snack bars were available along the river bank. How lucky he was to have this woman and this family!

His face relaxed in a wan smile, wondering what the difference was between Ah-Shan and those cute women who were articulate speakers. Chun'er, a young woman in his own village, was a canny one, but what had her shrewdness brought her? It was rather a type of dishonesty, which made her even poorer. Two months ago, when she heard a businessman was coming to the area to buy ginger, she sprayed water on her ginger that very night, hoping it would then weigh more. When the businessman arrived after a delay of several days, her ginger had begun to rot, and was refused.

The day he left for Wuluo, Chun'er put his hands in hers, crying her eyes out, because he had once promised to go to her parents with a proposal of marriage when he had enough money. Two years had passed since then, and he had gone to her with a woeful look on his face, saying, "It seems I will never have the money for a marriage. I can survive without money but you'll have to get married." Soon a matchmaker came to her, and another came to him. They were reluctant to part but they decided to go their own ways.

The day he left, her wedding date was still to be set. She walked with him on his way for some time to see him off, blaming him for being unfeeling, practical and spineless. He listened to her silently, wondering why she had agreed to marry a truck driver if she felt this way. Seeing him remain speechless, she stopped and growled through her teeth, "You've got to be careful. She may bear you a stupid son."

He was surprised because he had never thought about it. But what could he do? His parents had received a sum of money from Ma Gu to renovate his house for the first time. It was in such a bad condition that they had to put all their basins and bowls under the roof to collect water when it rained.

His father, who was blind in one eye, told him, "Think

before you leap. No turning back when you take that step. She will be your woman for life, even if she's crazy, foolish, crippled or blind. You've got to be nice to her."

He allowed himself a wry smile. He had not thought much about it, and he was not allowed to do so. It was as if a spark had fell onto his foot, and all he could do was to shake it off without considering anything else. He had to move forward step by step. It was impossible for him to look further and consider more. He knew for sure he had no other choice, unless he remained single all his life, spent no money and ate nothing but what he grew in the field. As a healthy, ordinary young man, he had to opt for a change. He was penniless now but he would soon earn more money. He considered himself lucky to now have a family and his own business without spending a penny of his own.

He thought he was doing the right thing. He was a newcomer to the town, and now he owned what even the locals longed for—a house, a store and more money to come. As a young man from a remote mountainous village, he had gotten all that he dreamed of overnight. Yesterday he took a bill from the till and hid it for himself, though he knew all the money he earned was actually already his money. He thought he should secretly stash away some money, a secret purse that the family knew nothing about. No one realized what happened regarding the shoe box contents, which encouraged him to continue. He had no idea why he did it, but he knew to have more money was a good thing.

Soon after Gaoshan opened for business, Ah-Shui went back to the city of Haishi, as she had achieved one of her ambitions. Ma Gu advised her daughter repeatedly, "Do your best with your new married life. You'll see it doesn't matter who your spouse is."

Ah-Shui said, "Yes."

Chapter Nine

Three months later, it was another early evening when Ah-Shui turned up again at the door. As she did the last time, she shouted "Mom!" before she moved to one side and said to the person following her, "Come on in."

All the people in the house expected Huang, the Haishi Man, only to find it was Qin Ziqing standing before them.

Ah-Shui soon explained to her mother what had happened.

"I felt sorry for him, Mom. If I had not gone to Haishi, he wouldn't have become what he is now. Do you know where he met his wife? When he learned where I went, he felt a twinge of envy and decided to go to the city himself to see what kind of place it was, and to persuade me to leave the guy from Haishi.

"He had a knife with him in his bag. He met a young woman on the train and started to tell her about his plan. She was so frightened that she tried to persuade him, speaking carefully, until she made herself a bit hoarse and dry-mouthed: 'Leave her alone, she's gone. If you love her, allow her do whatever she wants.'

"He didn't yield an inch, you know, until she said if he was a man, he should go and find the love of his life. 'You deserve true love and a better life than hers. She will come back to you with tears in her eyes.' Gradually he came to realize that he was not sure of his love for the woman called Ah-Shui. Maybe he felt shame, to be defeated by a stranger to the town.

"When he turned to look at the young woman talking to

him, he had a sudden feeling that she was practically born for him. Why should he risk his life to go after a woman when he was destined to meet another on his train?

"They talked continuously for the whole night until they got off the train at Haishi. He did not transfer to the long-distance bus to come see me, and the woman interrupted her planned journey. Together they enjoyed a hearty breakfast at the strange station before they boarded a return train.

"You see, it was because of me that he soon married the woman he met on the train, the wrong woman, one he thought he had fallen in love with at the first sight. It was an unhappy marriage; they couldn't get along although they tried to change. When we met last time I was back home, he made the decision, for the second time, to marry me. He went to Haishi after me and talked with my husband a couple of times. And we got divorced."

Ma Gu gave Ah-Shui a hard shove, "How foolish you are! You shouldn't have gotten divorced before he divorced his wife. What will you do if he can't get divorced?"

"He said he would take care of it. He told me not to worry about it. And I could actually care less."

"Just cut the crap!"

"Mom, you know what, he is somewhat like Dad. Do you know how great his plan is? All of you would be surprised if I tell you it's a major undertaking, the most miraculous project in the history of the town. The Five-Peak Mountain around us is so high that it prevents sunshine from coming in and for generations we've lived in the dark and damp. In winter the sun doesn't rise over the top of the hill until noon, and it disappears just when we realize it's there. It is cold and dark all winter. What life we are living here without sunshine? It looks like four or five in the afternoon when it is noon.

"We need a change but we all know nobody will come to help us. Our town is too small and remote to be remembered. Do you know a census is regularly done in other places? Is one done here in our town? Never ever! Nobody is interested in us and nobody knows how many people are living here. We have no choice but to help ourselves and save ourselves.

"So there is a group planning a project called 'Sunny Wuluo' to give us more sunshine. A huge mirror will be placed on the hill to reflect the sunlight down for the people here to enjoy. They presented numerous written reports to the local government until the authorities agreed, but no government funds have been given to support the project. The officials said the project could not be government one. It should be private charitable undertaking instead.

"Actually this project needs large sums of money. Experts in the city will be paid to discuss the design, and architects and engineers also have to be invited. They're still working on an exact budget, but they know it is a great deal of money and they have to manage it themselves. Qin Ziqing told me he had made up his mind to do it, even if he may go bankrupt for it."

Shaking her dumbfounded mother, Ah-Shui said, "Mom, we have the snack bar, so we might as well donate some money. This project is for the public good and everyone in the town will benefit from it."

Hearing the word "donate," Ma Gu seemed to awaken. She shoved away her daughter's hands.

"I would rather live without the sun than give money away."

Ah-Shui was upset. "We have too many people like you. That's why we're backward, forgotten and deserted."

"Who deserted us? We're safe and sound at the foot of Five-Peak Mountain! How can we be deserted? That's a downright lie!"

"It is really hard to get it to sink in with you. Anyhow you don't know what changes have happened outside since you limit yourself to this small world."

Some time later, the area known as Cloudy Slope, which had lain silent for years beside the town, suddenly became full of commotion—some people were running up and down it, and some were trying to look into a sort of instrument that stood on three legs, with their hips up in the air. Ma Gu wondered if they had discovered some treasure but then she focused on herself, thinking that her daughter, Ah-Shui, was among them. So she would get her share of the treasure if there was any.

When Ah-Shui managed to get home for dinner, she told her mother that the project was about to start and the exploration work had already began. When asked what the project was all about, Ah-Shui answered between mouthfuls, "I told you earlier: the sun and the glass. The glass will reflect sunlight. Why should we have a smaller share of the sunlight than the others?"

Before Ma Gu could ask more questions, Ah-Shui had pushed her bowl aside and run out with her mouth still full.

Raising her hand above her eyes, Ma Gu glanced at Cloudy Slope, where some people were busy with their hoes, as if they were scratching the hill's itches. Thinking about what Ah-Shui told her, Ma Gu could not help laughing to herself.

"To reflect the sunlight? The sun is high in the sky, and it gives and takes as it likes. How can you get what you want?"

It seemed that Ah-Shui was somehow involved in the project. Every morning she would freshen up hastily and then tap her way out. Together with two other girls who had been hired, she would stand with a bright red collection box out on the street. They said raising money was not the only purpose of theirs; they also wanted the locals to understand that the undertaking was a great deed, which was extraordinary significant to their lives.

Before long they achieved what they wanted. Villagers came up from all corners, gabbing and wrangling around the collection box.

"So, the winter in our town won't be as cold and the day will be longer?"

"But ... how can a single piece of cold glass change the weather? It is something I've never heard of."

"Are they lying? I heard stories about people going out to collect money during the day, but opening the box and pocketing the donations for themselves when they get back home."

"Yes, that's right. How can we know where the money ends up? Won't you misappropriate it?"

It saddened Ah-Shui to hear what the villagers said, but she was unable to argue with them. After many discussions, she took a long-distance bus to consult an expert. They decided to have a metal box made and fixed to a place in the downtown area with a blowtorch. There was no lock on the box, only a slit just wide enough for the donors to slip in their money. It was impossible for anyone to stick a hand in to get the money. On the day they launched the project, the donors would be called for a celebration and the collection box would be cut open.

Then a new doubt came up. Who would be responsible for the loss if someone took the box away at night? Ah-Shui noticed that Qin Ziqing, her lover, was wrinkling his brow, but she was sure he would come up with a solution. He was full of new ideas, and every time he raised his eyebrows, he would hit upon a good idea.

Several days later, a ladder was put up and a couple of workers fixed something that looked like a black box on a lamp-post. When asked they announced loudly, "This is a camera controlled by a computer. It records day and night whatever happens in front of it, like a security guard. It captures when someone puts money into the box and when someone bends to tie his shoelaces."

This idea was soon accepted by the villagers, but it was hard for them to adapt to the changed environment. They tried to skirt around the collection box and, when they had to pass by it, they would carry themselves stiffly to avoid reaching in the direction of the box or looking around in a suspicious manner, afraid that they would get themselves into trouble with the camera.

However there were organized groups that did not fear the black box. While it provided no funds for the project, the local government spared no effort in calling upon the townspeople to contribute to it. On every public holiday—Women's Day on March 8, May Day on May 1, Party Day on July 1, Army Day on August

1—processions of government employees were seen marching to the box with banners in their hands. When they were in front of the camera, they would subconsciously straighten their clothes and walk more solemnly, before they put their contributions into the box one by one. Levelheaded and sophisticated, they were frightened neither by television cameras nor by the black box on the post. Some of them even chose to smile for the cameras. Many people would wait to see the coverage on the evening news program when they were at the table for supper. They would be upset when they failed to see themselves, "I gave more than him, so how come he shows up instead of me?"

Soon it was the Hungry Ghost Festival, a time when Ma Gu would go with Little Yu to the riverside to burn paper money for her husband, Little Yu's maternal grandfather. On their way Ma Gu nagged and droned in the girl's ears, "I'm not afraid that he doesn't have enough money in the other world. I just want you to remember you have to do the same after my death, or your mother's or your aunt's. If you fail to do it, we will be poor and living a miserable life on the other side."

When they finished, Ma Gu sat down on the bank, motionless, gazing at the water.

"Granny, are you thinking about Grandpa?" Little Yu asked.

"Oh!" Ma Gu sighed. She was about to speak when a noise was heard in the water. It seemed as if someone was drowning. Wondering why someone was swimming when it was so late, Ma Gu felt rather frightened. After her husband's death, she had not allowed anyone in her family to swim in the river. She told them, "A couple of swimmers are killed every summer. Their souls are always crouching in the water, searching for scapegoats. They won't be reincarnated and will have to stay underwater unless they find someone to replace themselves."

As the sounds of splashing became louder, deep moans were vaguely heard. Petrified, Ma Gu asked Little Yu to hurry to the shore for help. Soon a group of villagers gathered on the bank. It was rather dark and they could see nothing in the river, but a couple of them jumped into the water without taking off their clothes and swam toward the center.

Others on the bank shouted out, "Hey, are you okay there?" A couple of torches swept over the water like searchlights.

After a noisy few moments they calmed down. Those Samaritans in the water began to complain, "Son of a bitch! Who was calling for help a moment ago? There is just a pair making love here! How dreadful it is! It is so cold and I have goosebumps all over."

Those on the bank started laughing and more voices rose up, "Where are they? Where are they? Give us more torchlight and let us see who they are."

The lights kept moving on the water, and more people were running towards them with torches in their hands. Soon the bank was lined with people and it seemed none of them meant to leave. The helpers swam slowly ashore, exclaiming while spitting on the ground superstitiously to drive away bad luck.

There seemed to be a couple in the middle of the water, floating and treading water sluggishly. Their clothes were discovered on the bank, bringing a volley of clamor, "Take them away and they'll have to walk home naked. They enjoy being together with nothing on, so let them."

In the swaying light beams of the torches, Little Yu vaguely saw a familiar face—Ah-Shui, her aunt. After some earnest observation she was almost sure that it was none other than Ah-Shui. Little Yu found herself too nervous to breathe properly. Grabbing hold of her grandmother's hand, she said softly, "Let's go home," but Ma Gu vigorously wrenched her hand free. Little Yu felt her grandma was shivering. Had she recognized her too?

After quite some time, all the villagers left, except Ma Gu, who was standing silently in the dark. The two lovers swam towards her slowly but their clothes had been taken away. They cowered and clambered over the shore, with their hands covering their private parts modestly, their teeth rattling like machine guns.

"Ah-Shui!" yelled Ma Gu out into the dark.

Ah-Shui was so frightened that she squatted down on the ground.

Ma Gu threw herself upon her daughter and slapped her violently in the face, before Little Yu realized what had happened.

Pulling Little Yu's hand, Ma Gu hurried up toward the street. After walking for a while, she said to Little Yu, "Go and fetch one of your coats." When the girl started to run, she called her to halt, "Never mind her and let her be!"

Back home Ma Gu gave a hard push to Little Yu, who was now stunned and pale.

"What's the matter with you? Why are you so numb and stupid?"

Her tears brimmed over and streamed down her cheek, as if a water bag had been pierced. But she could not tell her grandmother why she wept uncontrollably.

Chapter Ten

L ittle Yu was sleepless the entire night after Ah-Shui was found at the river. She had become aware of something she thought she had forgotten. It was upon hearing that strange sound that she was reminded. Yet she couldn't confide in Ma Gu as she was just a child in her grandmother's mind.

When the idea of learning to swim had occurred to Little Yu, there was no man in the family to guide her. So Ma Gu entrusted it to a neighbor who had been an itinerant carpenter. When Ma Gu's husband was still alive, the carpenter's artisanship and bright eyes deeply impressed him, and the man struck him as a promising carpenter. The carpenter was asked to stay and was recommended to the local wood factory. However Ma Gu's husband had a skeleton in his closet: he had been missing his son who died prematurely. If his son were still alive, he would be almost his age.

Later, when this man had his own easy life with a small family, he still kept in contact with Ma Gu, just like relatives, paying visits to each other on New Year's Day or during other holidays. Therefore Little Yu called him Uncle Wang.

Uncle Wang enthusiastically brought her to the river and reached his arms to support her tummy, as if holding the big tail of a frolicking fish. In no more than a single week, Little Yu learned how to swim!

"You are really smart," he said, stroking her hair as supple as seaweed.

On her tender and fresh face, the long eyelashes seemed as luxuriant and exuberant as growing rice shoots. Little Yu smiled mischievously and winked at him. She liked Uncle Wang a great deal, as he not only taught her swimming but also plucked lots of wild raspberries for her, making her lips terribly red. And he also bought her lollipops. With the light green end in her mouth and the stick hanging out, her cheeks swelled and bulged out. She enjoyed it every much. She had no money for lollipops; her grandma never gave her money, saying that children did not need money. Her first lollipop was from Uncle Wang who knew well that the girl liked the sweet, especially its light green top, even without asking. She felt Uncle Wang understood her far better than anyone else. Grazing on that lollipop, she walked from the streets to the riverside. For her, even the chance occasion of water choking her was pleasantly sweet.

When Uncle Wang tried to bring Little Yu to the middle of the river, she was so terrified that she shouted, "I won't! The water is too deep, I don't dare."

"I'm with you. What are you afraid of?"

Without asking her permission, Uncle Wang held Little Yu in his arms and swam toward the middle.

It was dusk. Slowly fog sprinkled itself from the sky, sprouted out of the trees, and rose from the ground. Very soon the heaven and the horizon were mixed and muddled in the distance. The swimmers went ashore for supper.

Little Yu said, "It's time for us to go home, otherwise, it'll be too dark for us to see."

Uncle Wang replied, "We might as well swim to the other side of the river and then walk home over that bridge."

Although a little bit tired, Little Yu was instantly excited by the idea of swimming through the deep part of the river to the opposite shore. Intent upon setting a new record, she spared no effort in swimming to make it across to the other side of the Wuhe River.

Before long they swam across the depths and drew near the shallows. As they were about to reach shore, Little Yu exclaimed excitedly, "Oh, my goddess, I made it across the Wuhe River! I made it!"

At that very moment, Uncle Wang leaned sideways, clasped her by surprise, and began to kiss her at random, rubbing and stroking her dainty and delicate torso. Flustered, she was choked by a bit of water, too scared to scream.

"Behave! Calm down!" he said. "Otherwise I will leave you alone here." Stealthily he took off his shorts. Little Yu was too alarmed and confused to swim away, holding his neck and letting him do as he liked. Without difficulty he stripped her of her bathing suit. Now she was totally at his disposal.

She felt something pushing aside her legs. A sharp pain made her gasp but she dared not utter another sound. A gigantic shame and fear repressed her. She dreaded being discovered by others or falling into a bottomless abyss to be engulfed and bitten to pieces by fish. She remembered seeing many drowned people, either without eyeballs or without noses. She wanted to run away but instead she hugged him close, as there was no other alternative.

Going ashore she tried to hide the physical pain so that nobody would notice the difference. Lowering her head she made her way crookedly and clumsily in front of him. The fog was now coming down. It wrapped her solidly like a mummy and escorted her home. She sensed that she mustn't tell Ma Gu. She knew well this was the last thing that Ma Gu would like to hear. Grandma was nagging in Little Yu's ears, "Virginity is of the greatest value and virtue." She knew the meaning of this utterance. But she had lost it at such an inexplicable time, lost this treasure in the river, and so had become valueless forever.

That evening it took Little Yu quite a long time to bathe. She felt she must be very dirty and she didn't know what he had put inside her. She even had the idea to cut herself open with a knife, to wash and flush herself, and then sew herself up. She did get a knife from the kitchen, but at the very moment the blade touched her, she came to her senses completely. She couldn't do it as it was too painful and dreadful. She threw down the kitchen knife. Bending over the basin, she began to sob softly. Since she could not cleanse herself, she thought, she had to conceal this secret. Weeping covertly she tried to recollect that awkward scene and was relieved there was nobody else at the riverside due to the enveloping fog.

That very night Little Yu developed a curious fever. There were no symptoms of catching a cold, just a fever. She lay on bed weakly, limp as a dead fish. At first Ma Gu took no notice, as she assumed her granddaughter was always well. She knew Little Yu even got over the dysentery that had been widespread earlier in the year, and believed it was a piece of cake for the girl to recover from small stuff.

After she returned home following a busy day's work, Ma Gu found Little Yu lying silently on bed. Reaching her hand to touch her, her grandmother was not so worried until she found Little Yu was as hot as food fresh from a steamer. She knew high fever was so dangerous that it could kill or at least be disabling.

She began to hurry and scurry everywhere. Superstitiously she got one of Little Yu's overcoat, held it high as a banner, and called out Little Yu's name while walking to and from along Little Yu's regular routes. But she could work no magic that day. After much trouble, nothing miraculous happened: the coat was still the coat, without gaining more weight. She realized she failed in this ritual; she had called back no spirit.

The trouble had nothing to do with the street, she decided. She remembered that Little Yu had gone to the river that day. Little Yu definitely must have lost her spirit in the river. Holding her granddaughter's coat, Ma Gu went to the riverside. After only several steps toward the river, she began to get a feeling. The coat in her hand seemed to be soaking with water, becoming heavier and heavier. Finally her arms were aching and too limp to support it any longer. Collecting and hugging the coat in her arms, as if holding Little Yu, Ma Gu made her way home shouting out, "Little Yu, let's go home! Go home with Grandma!"

This was not the first time that Ma Gu performed this magic. But this time even Ma Gu felt very curious and strange. Holding her granddaughter's coat, her nose began to twitch sharply and she found herself weeping after calling out her name two or three times. Touching and caressing her granddaughter's coat as if it was the girl's face, Ma Gu cried even louder.

The next day the fever came down, and Little Yu sat up in bed with her two sunken yet bright eyes fixed upon Ma Gu. "I dreamed of you last night," she claimed. "You were holding me in your arms with your tears dropping on my face." Ma Gu looked at her and could say nothing.

A few days later, Uncle Wang came for her. Standing at the door with a towel over his shoulder, he said to her, "Let's go to the riverside!"

Little Yu did not move as she did not intend to go with him, but she failed to come up with a reason to reject him. Smiling, Ma Gu took the peas from Little Yu's busy hands and urged her to go. "Go with Uncle Wang. Whatever you study, you do it well."

Little Yu had to stand up. Not daring to look back at him, she went ahead in a rush. He said repeatedly, "Slow down! Wait for me for a minute."

But she walked faster, made a sudden turn midway, and then started running toward an alley. She did not look back until she made a fair distance. Finding he was not following her, she started to go back slowly. She intended to stroll by herself in the streets until later. Then Grandma would not realize what had happened.

However he was waiting for her at the end of the alley! At the sight of him, she turned back in the other direction. He ran up to her and said, "If you keep away from me, I will tell your classmates what happened between us."

She paused, thought for a while, and followed him after all.

On her way home from school, she had to go by the gate to his house. One day just as she passed the gate, a hand popped out and seized her like a chicken before she had time to scream. His wife worked the whole day behind the counter of the local department store that featured products from the mountains, and he was working three shifts in the woodworking factory. That afternoon he was off, and his wife was, as usual, at work. Inside the house he placed Little Yu on the bed. He said to her, "I love you very much, really."

She wept continuously. He added, "I love only you in the whole world. Can you still remember when you were fenced in by your grandma as a child?

"Little Yu, the more I love you, the less I like other women. One day I will take you away. Really, this is how I feel. If you don't believe it, I can kill someone for you."

This statement reminded Little Yu of something. She stopped sobbing and asked, "Really?"

"Truly and completely."

All the days of being discriminated against and isolated at school came to mind. How she wished to give a beating to her classmate, the one who ranked second and who got the whole class to shun her. It would be enough to give her a good beating. No need to kill her. She revealed her idea to him.

"No problem," he said.

The next day, Number Two was knocked down by a bicycle and badly bruised. The rider got away without being identified as his hat was pressed down over his face.

That very afternoon the big hand reached out of the gate and dragged Little Yu inside again. "I did it for you," he said. "How will you reward me?"

Thinking for a short while, Little Yu set down her schoolbag and started to undo her trousers.

Later on he made her a schedule with some dates marked.

He would be at home those afternoons, and he hoped she would come to his house on her own, without his reaching out his hand. Otherwise he would go and meet her at school. He said he meant it.

What was strange was that gradually she did not fear or loathe him any longer. Many times when he scooped her up in his arms abruptly, she would spread her legs and wrap them around him as if he were a big tree to climb over. Jokingly he said to Little Yu, "You have got so much practice and training in this, you can graduate now."

When she was alone, she felt more loathing, especially of herself. Plainly there was another route for her to take. Even if he went to meet her at school, she could tell her teacher or the police, or she could even keep herself away from school. Every time she made her way to her teacher's office, every time she made her way to the police, she would halt and hesitate, and then run back. She didn't know what she was dreading or why she was hesitating.

Sometimes she would sit blankly in the darkness hoping he would disappear, without anyone aware of the truth. Maybe he would be hurt at work, or suddenly attacked by a serious illness, or taken away by the police for committing a crime. However he suffered from none of the above. On the contrary he enjoyed his daily life heartily. He had a spring in his step and would smile at Little Yu strangely.

Unexpectedly he was killed in a car accident. When she got the news, Little Yu was airing clothes with Ah-Shan on the balcony. She was struck dumb. She felt his death had something to do with her unspoken desires, and thought that someone invisible helped her achieve her wish. His ghost might have discovered the truth, or would know about it sooner or later, and was perhaps even gazing upon her reprovingly. All the other people went to see his corpse, broken and fragmented, his body bound up. Only Little Yu didn't dare.

Ma Gu said, "How can you behave this way? Do you

remember how Uncle Wang treated you while he was alive? How could a little girl be so cruel?"

But this was all just a dream. Little Yu was surprised that she should dream such a dream. There were even more surprises. After she woke from this weird dream, he came to tell her that he was setting up a woodworking factory, and he would be the boss.

Chapter Eleven

U ncle Wang's furniture factory opened for business.
   He delayed Little Yu and brought her to his office. He
put his hand on a wall, pushing until a crack opened up and she
saw inside a small room, in which there was nothing but a bed.
He said to her, "Look, this is my design. No one knows I have a
room here. It's our room."

When she came out of the room, he put his hand on the
hidden button again and the door closed slowly, leaving before
her a wall no different from any other wall in the room. She found
herself admiring Uncle Wang for his invisible button, wishing
she could have a similar one in her house, to allow her to live in a
world of her own, free from her granny's close observation.

Once in the room, he was nothing different from a dog,
kissing her all over from head to toe, although she tried to push
him away. Seeing tension building up in her, so that she was about
to burst open, he told her, "Little Yu, I have ripened you. When I
touched you the first time, you were like a young cucumber with
a small flower still on it."

He lifted her up to stand on the bed and began to stroke her
body as if she were made out of glass. He then whispered to her,
"You're mine, and you're not allowed to do this with anyone else.
Never do it behind my back. I tell you what, I will sense what has
happened if you do. And I will even smell it."

His kiss deepened and became hungrier. He ran his tongue

all over her, from her forehead to her thigh and all the way down to her toes. He sucked the deepest part of her small vagina. It seemed that he would have swallowed her whole. When he finally stopped, she stood up to look herself in the mirror. Terribly surprised to see the many red hickeys on her neck, she turned to stare at him, lying on bed, smoking.

He said with a charming smile, "Great. Those are my personal seals."

Covering her neck with her hands, she was afraid to go back home.

"Why don't you wear a scarf?" he suggested. He then went to pick up one for her, while she was waiting in the room.

With her new scarf around her neck, Little Yu had mixed feelings on her way home. It was early fall, and she must be the first person in the town to wear a scarf that year. It was a pink one, and she could read from the gaze of the passers-by how nice it was, but her face flushed with embarrassment. Years later when she counted how many scarves she owned, thinking over this hobby of hers, she realized she took it up that day. A scarf was not only a fashionable item, it also concealed her disgrace. She was ashamed of what she was doing but she knew deep down that she had come to love it. It puzzled her.

The next day she had to wear her scarf to school, as the marks on her neck were still clearly visible. When it was time for a sports lesson, the coach, who was also her math teacher, came to her and asked her to take it off.

"Little Yu, do you feel cold at this time of the year? You're not allowed to wear it in a sports class."

She removed it unwillingly after the teacher repeated what she had said three times. All around eyebrows rose in surprise. The teacher asked her solicitously what had happened. With great presence of mind, she told her they were marks left after a treatment of scraping therapy by her grandmother. However, the class teacher didn't believe what Little Yu said and called her aside.

"Tell me the truth, did you have the scraping therapy?" the class teacher whispered against her hair.

Little Yu didn't answer, thinking her class teacher must know what had happened. She thought it would probably be useless to lie, but she continued her story.

"Yes, I did. I had a sore tummy, and Granny did it with a copper coin."

Turning down her collar to have a closer look, after a while the class teacher said, "I don't believe these are bruises from scraping."

The class teacher left while shooting her a withering glance, which struck a chill in her heart. It was a look of contempt, scorn, mercy and everything.

In the small room, when Uncle Wang came to kiss her, she fought against him, saying, "The teacher didn't believe me. She said the marks were not left by scraping."

He didn't give in, and she struggled furiously but could not get away. All of a sudden, her shirt was ripped off. He shouted at her, "Big deal! We'll leave school. Will you still be afraid of her when we leave?"

He then buried his head in her neck and started to suck like a leech. She screamed shrilly with pain and pushed him away. Looking in a mirror, she saw numerous dark marks on her neck, which were bleeding slightly. They tingled when she touched them. Not knowing what to do about school the next day, she started to weep.

She refused to go to school the next morning. Lying in bed she told Ma Gu that she had a splitting headache and needed rest. Her grandmother agreed without a second thought. If the teacher came to visit her, Little Yu thought, she would go to school the next morning. She would do the same, even if one of her classmates was sent to her home instead of the teacher. Or she would sit up to tell her grandmother that she would go, if Ma Gu came to ask if she was feeling better or if she needed to write an excuse for her absence from school. A day passed but neither someone from the school nor her granny came to her. This left her desperately disappointed.

On the third day, she was still waiting for her last opportunity. It was enough for her, she thought, if Ah-Shan entered her room and asked why she didn't go to school. She would pretend to awaken and would leap out of bed for school when Ah-Shan approached. She waited in vain. Arriving home from the snack bar, Ah-Shan started doing laundry and knitting before she was completely exhausted and collapsed into a chair, snoring noisily.

She dawdled to her school the fourth day. But she was stopped by the teacher before reaching the classroom.

"Do you think a school is a vegetable garden where you come and go freely? Why didn't you send a note?"

She was punished by having to stand on the sports field while the other pupils were having their classes. During the break between classes, a group of curious students came to see what had happened to her. She was about to leave herself when the teacher came and asked, "Well, who said you can leave now? Did I say it?"

She could do nothing but remain standing there. When the second session was over, she saw her teacher come out of her office, walk through the sports field, and go out of the school gate.

"Has she forgotten all about me?" Little Yu thought.

She had indeed forgotten that the girl was on the field. The last session of the morning was about to end, but Little Yu was still standing under the harsh sun. She was streaming with sweat and the heat made her feel faint. Maybe she could pretend to crumple into a heap on the floor, leaving the teacher to regret her decision for physical punishment. But the teacher was not in the school. When she was wondering what to do, she heard the bell for the end of the last session. Unconsciously she turned and started to move. She could not stand the derisive laughter from her schoolmates, which would follow. She didn't know what would happen but she must leave now.

She left the school forever. Meeting her on her way, Uncle Wang said he had seen that she was made to stand on the field.

"Why do you have to go to that damn school? I would have left, if I were you," he said. "We'll have to leave the school. I'll pay for you to go to a school in a big city soon, when I make a profit," he continued.

Her eyes brightened, "You really mean it?"

"I mean it. There are much better schools."

All of a sudden, her face was glowing with happiness, and she tore the school badge off her sweater.

Chapter Twelve

Little Yu's decision to leave school came as a great shock to the whole family.

"What on earth did you do?" Ma Gu asked.

"If you don't tell me the truth, you've got to go with me to your teacher," Ah-Shui threatened.

Even Ah-Shan greeted her idea with scorn, "What's the difference between a kid and a pig, if the kid doesn't go to school?"

Little Yu remained silent until Ah-Shui grabbed her by the arm to drag her to school. Little Yu started screaming, "Who says I hate school? I hate the school in this town but I'll go to a school in a big city. I'll leave this place."

She was about to rush out but Ah-Shui was quick enough to seize her arm to hold her back.

"A school in a big city? That's easy for you to say, but do you have the money? Tell you the truth, if you think I am going to support you, you can think again. I won't give you a penny."

"You're flattering yourself! I don't need your lousy money. I'll work for my tuition fees," Little Yu answered with confidence.

Uncle Wang had promised her a job in the store where his wife worked. Little Yu was half afraid to take it, but he said, "Don't worry. There's nothing to be afraid of. The most dangerous place is the safest one. I'm sure she'll never know unless you tell her yourself. She helped in securing the job for you."

Little Yu had no idea when her attitude toward Uncle Wang

changed. She had thought she hated him, and she had chosen not to report him to the police only because she would feel ashamed when it was made public. But everything had changed, and she knew deep down that she liked it when he had sex with her. She could have taken a circuitous path on her way back from school to avoid having to pass before his gate, but she didn't. She pretended to be afraid of encountering him and feigned struggle when he held her by the arm. She would take the same road the next day in spite of herself.

One day she broke a pot for pickling vegetables and felt deeply ashamed when her granny screamed at her. She ran out crying, wondering where she could go. She grew up in the town but she had no close friends in the neighborhood. Walking up and down the street helplessly, she thought of him. She went up to knock at his door. She began to weep when the door opened.

Learning what had happened, he said with a smile, "It isn't the end of the world! I'll bring a pot to your granny tomorrow. I have too many them."

Hearing what he promised, her tears gave way to laughter. As usual he had sex with her. When they finished he told her, "Little Yu, we can't go on like this. I can't see you any more. I'll have to move to a place farther away from where you live."

"No, you can't," she responded instinctively.

He gazed at her for a while and then cupped her face in his hands.

"You're a grown-up now and you know what love really means."

He didn't leave dark love bites on her neck anymore. He chose her breasts, inner thighs and other locations, where they were not seen easily.

"You're afraid your wife would see them? She'll know all about it, if I ever make a slip of the tongue."

He said with a smile, "I'm glad you're no longer a little girl."

However she could no longer go out without a scarf around her neck, feeling uneasy exposing her bare neck. At the same time, a thin scarf created some distance in her life, giving a feeling of being shy and retiring. She loved what he did, in the small stuffy room, to turn her on. Instead of stripping her stark naked like a beast, he would peel off her clothes slowly, piece by piece, as if unwrapping a precious gift. After the scarf was finally removed, he would scoop her into his arms and press her to his chest, as he would hold a bird gently in his palm, which filled her with much more happiness than the marks all over her.

He was pleased to know how obsessed she was with scarves, bringing her different types as gifts. To his delight what she loved was a scarf, not jewelry and dresses. He could afford any scarf available in town, and she found more and more of them in her bedroom closet.

Chapter Thirteen

Little Yu had never expected to meet Gao at Uncle Wang's office. She forgot that Uncle Wang had his takeaway box lunch sent to him from the little snack bar, Gaoshan, and that Gao delivered it. That day Gao stopped when he entered the office, his mouth half open as if he had a hot dumpling in it to chew before swallowing. She was about to laugh before she realized she was sitting on Uncle Wang's lap. The factory was closed for the day and there were no workers around, so Uncle Wang had started to kiss and fondle her.

Gao stood motionless, as if he had forgotten why he was there. Uncle Wang rose to take the lunch from him. He rubbed his nose and said with a smiling face, "She comes to visit very often. I took her out for some fun, like a father, when she was little."

Without a word, Gao took out a dirty notebook, opened it and placed it on the desk before him. Uncle Wang never paid in cash; he signed his bills for later payment.

Putting his notebook into his pocket, Gao looked into Little Yu's eyes and said, "It's time for you to go home for lunch."

It was the first time he had spoken to her in a tone of command. Actually he was silent at home, seldom involving himself in conversation. The way he looked at her was also different. It seemed he was coldly angry.

Little Yu was thinking she should quarrel with Gao before

he left, so she could blame him for framing her when he told her grandmother what happened in the office. But Uncle Wang told her to go back home.

"I'm sorry I didn't know you were coming, so I didn't get you any lunch."

She had no intention to leave, and she was disappointed that Uncle Wang did not support her by warning Gao not to tell anyone about what he saw. Thinking he didn't want her to stay, she answered coldly, "I don't want to eat your damn food!"

Little Yu walked along in a huff, and Gao followed.

"I think you'd better not to go to his place," he said. She kept silent. "I know straight off he's not a good guy," he continued.

She challenged him in a muffled voice, "Yeah, you're a good guy, and all others are bad ones."

"I'll tell you about him for your own good. Believe me. I know he has designs on you," he continued.

He then seized her hands and asked her to look him straight in the eye. She did, and this time she saw a pair of warm eyes rather than cold ones. Immediately she looked away but she knew he was staring at her. She blinked disdainfully as an answer to his fixed gaze. But he didn't avert his eyes from her face. She turned violently to look him in the eye.

"Don't stare at me!"

"I'm trying to read the expression on your face to see how you resemble your father."

"Stop it. He's a much better man than you."

"You don't say? So why did he run away and leave you behind? He has no sense of duty, does he?"

"Don't speak ill of him behind his back! You're nothing compared with my dad," Little Yu replied before she started to run. It was the first time that the words "your father" were mentioned in front of her, and no one had ever said her father had no sense of duty. She had never seen her father and she had no idea what kind of man he was. But it puzzled her that she was on his side when someone was trying to belittle him.

After a considerable lapse of time, Little Yu was sure that Gao didn't tell the family about what he saw in Uncle Wang's office. She wondered why he kept it a secret. Anyhow it was not much of a secret, she thought. It was not a big deal for her to sit on Uncle Wang's lap, as everyone in the family knew he liked her ever since she was a little girl. He took her swimming, walked into the hills to pick plums for her, and caught eels with her in the stream. She even hoped Gao would tell the family about it, so she could see how they would despise him rather than applauding him.

Several days later a visitor approached the snack bar. Gao greeted her with a smile while she was still outside. She was a gorgeous woman, and at a quick glance Little Yu was convinced she was as beautiful as Ah-Shui, "Miss Wuluo" herself, although less fashionably dressed. Going with her to Ma Gu, Gao introduced her in a cheerful voice, "This is Chun'er, my cousin on my father's side."

Hearing that Chun'er was a relative of Gao, Ma Gu became genuinely friendly, plying her with questions. Gao stood staring at Chun'er with bewilderment, but she ignored him, giving Ma Gu ready answers. She told Ma Gu that her mother and Gao's father were the only children of her grandparents, and that she and Gao had been as close as brother and sister since they were kids. She said she was in town to visit a dealer of turmeric, a Chinese herbal medicine.

"I dropped by to see my cousin, his wife and you," she told Ma Gu in her honeyed tones, which pleased Ma Gu. Several times Little Yu noticed Chun'er shooting a withering glance at Ah-Shan, but Ma Gu was so excited that these actions didn't register. With a smile Ma Gu told Gao to leave his work aside for the rest of day and show Chun'er around the town. Gao was pleased and left immediately after he removed his apron.

Gao and Chun'er came back cheerfully, rather late at night, when Ma Gu was about to go to bed. Chun'er said she had visited the medicine dealer and they reached an agreement. She also told

Ma Gu that next month she needed her cousin to go with the dealer to her village, because the dealer had no idea how to get there. Ma Gu agreed readily to that plan.

As a guest had come to visit, Ah-Shui was called to return and join them. At the dinner table, Gao asked Ah-Shui how much money had been collected for the project. Ah-Shui said no one would know until the collection box was cut open at the opening ceremony.

She paused before she continued, "Well, I think it's almost full. When I donated again a couple of days ago, I had to shove my notes in. It was different when I did it the first time—I could feel the money falling down to the bottom. By the way, the government has encouraged people to donate, and several big events have been held to raise money. Television cameras were invited, and the government men donated hundred-yuan bills in front of the cameras to appeal for more donors."

"I think I need to go and donate. I've become somewhat of a local now," Gao said.

Ah-Shui brightened up immediately and nodded her agreement, "Yes, you're right. Everyone in the town should contribute, especially small businessmen like you. You know what, schoolchildren gave what they had in their piggy banks. You're adults and you should know better than to be stingy."

Ma Gu didn't speak a word, as she had never thought of giving. Then she retorted, "It's enough that you donated; you did it for our family."

Ah-Shui could do nothing about her mother, who she knew was very tight with her money. She ran a snack bar but she had never provided a free breakfast for the committee of the "Sunny Wuluo" project, while owners of many other businesses willingly offered what the committee needed free of charge. Ah-Shui was ashamed of her mother for her stinginess, but Ma Gu had a plausible explanation, "Why do you expect me to do something when my daughter is already helping without being paid?"

Probably because they were talking about charity, the

conversation between Ah-Shui and Gao went on amicably. They turned the topic from how to cut open the collection box to the security camera installed for it.

"Does it work around the clock? Do they have a record of what happens at anytime of the day?"

Ah-Shui took a glance at him before she said, "Well why do you ask? I think so, but I know nothing about cameras to be honest. No one bothered about it after it was set up."

Rubbing her shoulders with her hand, Ma Gu curled her lips in a contemptuous sneer and said to Gao, "It's none of your business. You leave it alone. Someone must be in charge of it because the project is a big one."

For some time, Ma Gu had complained of a pain in her shoulders, rubbing them or stretching her arms in the air whenever she had the time. One day when she was doing it, her arms stopped in the air suddenly and she murmured to herself while staring into space, "Good heavens! Is a flood coming?"

She felt a gloomy foreboding, like when the floods hit her village many years ago and washed her ashore in this small town—her eyelids kept twitching and then she became so dizzy and light-headed for no apparent reason that she had to lie still on the bed.

Ah-Shui rejected her mother's idea, "Stop being superstitious! It's nothing but dizziness, or Meniere's Disease in terms in Western medicine."

Ma Gu was upset, wondering how it could be that she was not psychic. She believed that, as a woman who differed physically from most others, she had hidden systems all over, which helped her pick up signals from the gods.

Chun'er cut in, "That reminds me of what happened in my village recently. The monkeys in the mountain were nowhere in sight, simply vanishing without a trace, but masses of snakes were seen in the fields, on roads, in trees, and even in kitchens. They were everywhere. The villagers believed something would go wrong."

It seemed she was entreating Ma Gu for a mysterious solution. However Ma Gu answered indifferently, "It meant nothing for the monkeys to disappear from view. There were tigers around but do you see a tiger now? We had primitive savages but we never hear of them now. There were large trees in the mountains as thick as several men belted together, but it's news now when you see a tree that takes two men to put their arms around."

Chun'er tried to stick to her topic, "A type of strange, long, dark pine worm was also found. They cling to trees, looking no different from tree branches. When you shake the tree, they fall to the ground like sausages. When these worms are on a tree, the leaves fall gradually and the tree dies."

All the people in the room were frightened.

"Those are weird!"

Ah-Shui continued, "Yes, they are. I heard a power station was built somewhere downstream and a dam cut the Yangtze River in the middle. The water rose more than a hundred meters. Countless hills were underwater and landslides smashed into villages."

"What happened to the villagers?" Ma Gu was eager to know.

"Many left before the water rose, but some unwilling villagers refused to leave and had to struggle in the water. A few of them left at the very end, carrying on their back a tree they dug out of the slope behind their houses."

"Our town won't flood, will it?"

"Nonsense. Half of China would be underwater if our town were to flood. This place is so high that a car takes thirty-six turns before it reaches the top of Five-Peak Mountain."

Gao said, "You may be wrong. Water takes no turn when rising. It comes as quick as fire."

"Do you really wish for our town to disappear one day like those villages? Don't you think you're like a local now?" Ah-Shui stared at Gao, looking as if her feelings had been hurt.

Little Yu was woken up by a strange noise in the dead of

night. In bed with her eyes wide open, she tried to decide what it was. It was from the sitting room where Chun'er slept, and it seemed that someone was weeping for a while and then giggling, with occasional breaks of talking. She crept from her bed to see what was happening, looking through a crack in the door. Gao sat face to face with Chun'er, who had a handkerchief in her hand. It seemed she was sobbing. Gao kept his head low but he looked up to whisper to her from time to time.

The next day Little Yu told Uncle Wang what she had seen during the night. He said, "I don't know if she's his cousin but I saw them with my own eyes making their way down a street, hand in hand. Do cousins hold hands? I have a female cousin but I never touched her hands when I was with her. It must be Ah-Shui that was the problem. She has broken up a couple of lovers. I was sure she would shoot herself in the foot sooner or later."

Chun'er was leaving, and Gao went to the bus station to see her off. She had two large bulging plastic bags in her hands. In one of them were used clothes and bedding that Ma Gu gave her—two and a half sets of bed sheets, a woolen sweater with a loose collar, two pairs of leather shoes with broken heels, and a number of colorful dresses made from man-made fibers. Many of them were from Ah-Shui's closet. In the other were spring rolls, twisted rolls and rice balls with sesame that Ah-Shan prepared for her. Following them from far away, Little Yu suddenly felt an overwhelming desire to see what they looked like when walking hand in hand, wondering if she needed to confirm what Uncle Wang said about them or to expose something.

When they were approaching the station gate, Chun'er stopped suddenly. Little Yu paused to hide herself from them.

"Come on. Hold on a little longer. We're about there," Gao said.

Throwing one of the bags on the ground, she shouted at him, "What does she think I am? A pack rat? I would rather go around naked in my house than to wear these handouts she gave me." She was so worked up that she kicked at the bag on the ground.

"Why not? You brought them all the way here. It's a good idea to give them to some people in your village."

She pushed him so hard that he almost lost his balance as he was about to pick up the bag. They stood face to face for a while, their eyes locked together, before she threw herself into his arms. After an initial shock, he pushed her away, but she struggled into his arms. He gave up, allowing her to put her arms around his waist.

Little Yu felt a sudden urge to walk up and pass right before them, to see how Gao would react.

She walked out of her hiding place. Raising his head up, Gao met Little Yu's eyes and went crimson with embarrassment, gazing at her open-mouthed over Chun'er's shoulder.

Without a word Little Yu left. She turned her head back twice. First she saw Gao taking his hands off Chun'er and looking at her empty-handed as if she had grabbed something from him. Then she spotted Chun'er turning to stare at her. The two of them kept their eyes glued to her face, appearing lost and lonely, like two kids who had been suddenly deprived of their toys.

Soon Gao caught up with Little Yu. She was not going back to the store where she worked. Instead she was headed to a porcelain kiln, so that she could tell them not to deliver any new items. These would normally be packaged for them as soon as they were moved out of the kiln, according to the contract. But the products were not selling well, and her store was still full of them. That had happened ever since a lot of new porcelain products were introduced into the market. Compared with the heavy local types covered with dark spots like freckles, the new ones were thin and light, as if made from glass.

"Can I go with you?" Gao said.

She ignored him, but he walked beside her. Actually she was not against his suggestion. The kiln was not very far away, but she had to go via a mountain road. She feared nothing but the well-fed, large guard dogs the villagers kept, which would come out from nowhere, barking furiously as if they wouldn't stop until they had broken her legs.

"Chun'er is getting married. She wept because her husband's home is too far away from hers," Gao told Little Yu.

"I know you're a better choice for her."

"Do you know what you're talking about?"

"Uncle Wang has the same idea." She had never thought she would mention Uncle Wang unless Gao brought up the subject.

"Let me tell you. I won't tell anyone about your affair with Uncle Wang, and you keep secret what you saw just now. Okay?"

She had not thought of letting anyone on to his secret. However as soon as his words escaped his lips, an idea hit upon her that she could ask him for something in exchange for this deal. She had no idea right now what she might need, but she felt a window of opportunity had been created for her. She would have to see for what she might exchange the secret.

She rolled her eyes as her mind moved in quantum leaps, manipulating ideas and jumping on to new ones. She thought of a scarf but discarded it immediately, as it was too small an item for such a big secret. A dress was not valuable enough either, she thought, and she had no idea what to buy. She was searching her mind when she caught sight of a girl in front of her, who was in a school uniform, wandering along the street. It was a school day, so Little Yu was sure the girl must have played hooky for the day. Then she suddenly remembered her own plan for schooling. Uncle Wang promised her the tuition fees, but it would be better for him if Gao could share them.

She told Gao without any hesitation, "What about a sum of money? For my schooling in the city. I'll keep it a secret if you give me the money."

"This is blackmail. I'm your father by law."

"Actually you're neither my father nor my mother's husband."

Standing motionless he realized how he had underestimated the quiet girl. She was highly sophisticated, but he had thought she was a pure and innocent teenager. Now he understood she was even more sophisticated than he was.

"What if I have no money. Your granny manages all the money from the snack bar, you know. I don't have a penny."

"I'll give you two months before you have to give me the tuition fees for the first year of my school. That's not too much, is it? You're my stepfather. It's your duty to do it."

He didn't move, looking at her as she walked away. He murmured to himself, "My money for you? No way!"

He lived in constant fear of being discovered for stealing from the shoe box, and he had finally found the safest place for his money. He bought a package of tobacco for his father, put the bills in the largest leaf without Chun'er knowing it, and told her to give to him. No one would trouble themselves to touch his father's tobacco leaves, but his father would see the money when he spread the leaves out carefully to wet them with saliva, as he always did before he rolled his own cigarettes.

"I have, at long last, about a thousand yuan. Why should I give it to her?" he whispered to himself.

Chapter Fourteen

It seemed soon everyone in the town was talking about how Ah-Shui had sex with her poor first love in the river. They identified the two easily by what they found in their pockets—his work permit and her key ring with her picture in a tiny plastic box. They may not have known her name but they were familiar with her lovely face.

The donations were being collected in the official name of "Sunny Wuluo," but the affair between Ah-Shui and her lover almost ruined the project. Rumors were going around that the activity was a big con by which the shameless man and woman were amassing a huge fortune for themselves. Some of the donors even suggested cutting the collection open before the ceremony to get their money back. A large group of them staged a sit-down protest in front of the town government's office, because the government had encouraged them to give to a couple of adulterers.

"Does the government promote adultery?"

"Does it encourage cheating in a name we've never heard of?"

"Why should we trust these people who have absolutely no morals?"

They claimed both the charity project and the government had betrayed the trust of the townspeople. They could only trust their money and they wanted it back. They had the right to spend it on drinks if they were happy about it.

The babble of argument continued for quite a long time before a couple of grim-faced men walked out of the gate. The one in the middle started to make a speech, "The Sunny Wuluo project has nothing to do with what those two people did. They may have done something inappropriate, but their project is a philanthropic project as well as an act of charity. It was discussed from many perspectives before it was launched. It's a mistake to confuse the one with the other.

"Let me give you an example. It may be the case that you didn't honor the elderly in your family as you were expected to, cheated on your wife, or walked away with something from your neighbor's house. But the rice you grow isn't guilty, because it remains what it is, even if you, the grower, has done something wrong."

His example set everyone in the audience off laughing, and the strained atmosphere was lightened. The man then continued, "You're lucky to have me here because I know what you have on your mind. But the police would have being called to come if someone else was talking to you today. Why? Because you're here with weapons. It's radically different when you're armed in a protest, you know."

As his words fell from his lips, the so-called arms were being put away under the carriers' coats. They had never thought their tools to open the collection box—kitchen knives, chain saws and the like—were weapons in the eyes of the government. They were frightened out of their wits, because all they wanted was to open the box and get their money back, not to kill anyone. Of course they knew they would be unable to force the box open with those simple tools, but they had them in their hands to show their determination.

They finally stood up, one after another, and headed back. While they walked, they talked to one another, "Come on. It's not that easy to deal with the government. You may be mistaken. Weapons? They are never fun. You may be put into jail and get killed. Who would die for that money we donated?"

The Sunny Wuluo committee decided to start work on the project ahead of schedule. They believed a sunnier and brighter town was the best medicine for the doubts and anger felt by the donors. It was also the only way to save the project and Qin Ziqing, its director, whose reliability had dwindled away to nothing.

The crisis of confidence facing Sunny Wuluo was becoming less serious, but Ah-Shui was once again under a spotlight in the town. Her own family was dishonored when she ran away with Haishi Man, but this time another woman and her family had been caught up in the adulterous affair. Ma Gu was sure something would happen. She had waited for it for too long, and was on tenterhooks day and night.

Ma Gu hired a couple of rural types, who worked noisily to replace her wood windows with steel ones and added two extra iron sheets to her door. The house was much darker inside and looked like a birdcage. When the workers left, with a long breath of relief, Ma Gu sat herself comfortably into her old wicker chair and raised her teacup to her lips.

"It's done. At least I'm no longer afraid of unexpected bricks in my house," she said to herself.

One rainy evening Ma Gu was busy making the third round of green tea for the day when there was a loud knock at the door. She asked in alarm who it was, and the voice said, "I'm here to read your electricity meter."

Ma Gu went to turn the knob without giving a second thought. The doors opened and a woman barged in. She was thin and short, but her delicate face was twisted with rage, her eyes bulged, her arched eyebrows danced like the twitching tongue of a venomous snake, and her slack mouth turned pale and contorted with emotion.

Pointing at Ma Gu with her forefinger, she screamed, "That shameless daughter of yours! Where are you hiding her? Tell me where is she! I won't leave until I see her."

She banged her fist angrily on the table before she threw

herself into the wicker chair in which only Ma Gu sat. Ma Gu looked at the woman nervously, as if fearing her favorite chair would collapse under the woman's weight. Ignoring the expression on Ma Gu's face, the woman twisted violently in the chair and thumped her fist down on the table with each of her sentences, leaving the tea in Ma Gu's pot dancing as if it was frightened. With an even louder cry, her arm jerked, spilling the tea out. The pot rolled on the table and fell onto the floor, leaving broken pieces all over.

Suddenly the room went entirely quiet. After a while Ma Gu reached down to pick up the splinters, piling them up in her hand. She hesitated suddenly before she reached her hand out toward a piece lying at a foot of the woman, who was wearing black leather shoes and white socks. As she shouted, her feet moved up and down, looking like terrified doves. Ma Gu's hand kept trembling slightly, and she was about to grasp the splinter, when one of the "doves" was frightened and flew off. It hit itself hard on Ma Gu's head and bounced back to the floor. With a muffled cry Ma Gu fainted away.

As if she needed to explain her violence, the woman jumped up from the chair and shouted in anger, "Whoever helped her has to be punished! I'll come again and again until I see her."

While speaking she walked backwards to open the door. When Little Yu arrived with a kitchen knife in her hand, the woman was already outside. Ma Gu rushed over to hold Little Yu's legs tight.

"Come on. Run! Get out!" Little Yu threw the knife at the woman, who screamed shrilly. Fortunately the knife hit the iron door and fell on the ground with a sharp noise, producing a couple of flying sparks.

Little Yu was weeping, but Ma Gu said, "I'm frightened to death, you silly girl. You would be put into jail if you kill her, and you'd be killed. It was silly of you to do that. That was a rather foolish thing to do. I know you were trying to protect me because you love me. But you've got to put yourself in the woman's place.

Your aunt hurt her; it was all Ah-Shui's fault. If I were her, I would have done the same."

Little Yu raised her head when she saw a tiny puddle forming beside her, only to find Ah-Shan standing there with her mouth half open, her eyes looking into space. Dropping her eyes, Little Yu realized the puddle was under Ah-Shan's feet. She was so frightened that she had wet herself.

The next day a sticking plaster was seen on Ma Gu's forehead. She went to the snack bar quietly, as if nothing had happened the previous night. She told Little Yu, "Now I won't worry any more. She'll stay away from us and she won't trouble Ah-Shui. People depend on breath. When she let out a long breath to give vent to her anger, she wilted like a leaf in a heat."

She then warned Little Yu not to tell her aunt about it, "It'll get worse if she finds out."

Chapter Fifteen

Uncle Wang was about to celebrate the first anniversary of his factory.

It was an event Little Yu had been waiting for silently, as he had promised to give her some of the money he received as congratulatory gifts.

Following a group of guests, Little Yu came to the factory. She saw Uncle Wang walking among the visitors in a suit and tie, his face suffused with color. Beside him was a noisy woman who wore a lot of makeup. She supposed that she must be his secretary and office manager.

The guests were all gone, and the loud noise of firecrackers was no longer heard, leaving red remains all over the ground. Baskets of flowers stood in two lines creating a passage at the front of the factory gate. Some of the flowers in the baskets drooped, and the ribbons with names of the guests flew in the wind. It seemed those gifts were like traditional Chinese opera performers, who would nod off to sleep in the yard of an open theatre, costumes unbuttoned, when the audience left.

Little Yu lurked behind a tree, looking into the room through a large, new window made from aluminum, as if she was watching a movie. It was getting dark, but Uncle Wang, along with a couple of other people, was busy with something, moving around in the room occasionally. Keeping her eyes glued on them, she suddenly felt Uncle Wang was such a stranger to her that it seemed he lived in a different world, one that was beyond her reach and had nothing to do with her. He appeared a different person when he was with his men. Wondering which was his true self, she told herself the illusion must be a matter of distance. It would disappear when she was standing before him or sitting on his lap when they were alone later that day. She felt he was a stranger because she had never looked at him from such a long distance.

Their work finished, his men walked out of the room one after another, speaking to each other loudly, and their steps faded into the distance soon after they were outside the gate. Little Yu was about to enter the room when Uncle Wang came out with his suit jacket hanging loosely over his shoulders. She tiptoed quietly and stood before him without saying a word. He was surprised to see her.

"Why are you here?"

"I've been around for a long time but I didn't come in because you weren't alone."

"Did they see you?" he asked while looking around nervously. She shook her head.

He thought for a moment before he open the door for her.

"Why are you here? I didn't ask you to come. I had a busy day and it's time for a breather now."

As he didn't mention his promise to her, she plucked up enough courage to ask him about it.

"You told me to come. You promised me. Have you forgotten about my school in the city and the money for it?"

"No, no, how could I? Unfortunately those guests were stingy. They came with a lot of baskets of flowers but not much cash as gifts for me. And it's in my secretary's hands not mine."

"But she does what you say!"

"No, you're wrong. As the saying goes, a sparrow may be small but it has all the vital organs. Even this factory has rules, and no one is allowed to misuse funds."

"What can I do then? You said it yourself. You said you

would give me the money for a school in the city."

Looking at Uncle Wang, who seemed to be a changed man, she felt she was sinking to the depths of despair, as if she was helplessly alone in a dark room.

"Yes, I promised you but sometimes things happen in ways we never expected. They go their own way, you know. Now I can only say I'll try my best to help you."

She started to sob uncontrollably. "So why did I listen to you in the first place? I don't want to drop out. I want to go to school."

"But that's not my fault. You know I didn't drag you away from your school. That was your own decision."

"I would never have dropped out, if you hadn't promised me."

"Do you know what you're talking about? Do you still remember what I told you the day you left school? I said you should think again before you make that big decision. You said you had decided to leave your school. Didn't you say you don't have to go to school because many people live a good life without going?"

"That was my assumption. I only meant in case I wasn't able to go to a school in the city."

"And now you know sometimes things happen in the most unwanted way."

Her sobs turned into wails. Sitting beside her, Uncle Wang got pretty upset.

"Stop that weeping and wailing. I didn't mean it's impossible. Let's see what I can do sometime in the future, okay? I'm sure I'll make a big fat profit when this shipment of products is sold. And I'll do what I promised. It'll be a piece of cake. You'll see."

While she was crying, Little Yu was going over what Aunt Lu, Uncle Wang's wife, had told her, "You can never believe what a man says when he's getting drunk, soothing an upset woman, or comforting a woman whose feelings are hurt, unless he writes it down for you."

To her own surprise, she suddenly blurted out, "Why don't you write it down for me, saying you'll give me the money for school when the shipment is sold."

"What? Why should I? I owe you nothing, Little Yu. Do you think I owe you something? No, I don't owe you anything. We love each other. You've been with me all these years without anyone forcing you. Right? We owe each other nothing."

She began to weep again, but he continued, "I'm disappointed in you. Write it down for you? You're young, so where did you learn these tricks? You were different but you've changed so much in a short time. I'm really disappointed in you."

She sobbed all the harder. She felt deeply wronged by his blaming her, and he was doing it again but there was nothing she could do about it. He said, "Well, if that's so, I guess we don't have to see each other again. Your criticism is too much for me, so I'll leave you alone. Good luck!"

He was ready to leave as he finished his words. She hoped he would come over to hug her, as always. If he did, she would forgive him and agree to wait for the money, instead of insisting on having him write his promise down.

Without the intention to go to her, he stood by the door waving his hand to motion her to leave. Seeing she remained motionless as a log, he moved peevishly to her. Holding her with his fingers by her sleeve, instead of her hand, he said, "Come on. It's getting late. My wife thinks I'm cheating on her when I'm back home too late."

"We were out much later when we met. Why didn't she get suspicious then?"

"You're different now, different from how you were. I wonder why you're so ... so mean."

"I'm not, but you've changed and broke your promise."

"I'll tell you again, I didn't promise you anything. I have no right to tell you what you should do. I'm not your father. Why would you have to do what I say? Don't you have a mother? Nobody will believe what you say anyhow."

When they were turning onto a main street, where there were more people, he said, "I'll go first, and you go home yourself."

He was several steps ahead of her before she understood what he meant.

Chapter Sixteen

The day the collection box was to be opened, it turned out to be clear and sunny.

The villagers were not expecting a sunny day. At about eight o'clock the town remained cloaked in a thin mist, looking as if it was still half asleep. This was not an exception. It had been an established routine for the villagers to wonder in the early hours of the morning whether the sun would be coming out, a few spots of rain would fall, or it would be suffocatingly dark and gloomy all day long. Ma Gu was always saying, "My town is hated by the heavens."

It was past nine and the villagers around the collection box were about to leave when a yellow sun suddenly emerged from behind a peak. The mist vanished unwillingly, like a cobweb in a strong wind, leaving the crowd on the central square cheering loudly in the sunny town.

Qin Ziqing elbowed his way through the crowd and strutted towards the collection box. Moving nearer to a microphone in his red coat, he announced loudly the launch of the Sunny Wuluo project. He had an electric cord, probably for the blowtorch, in his hand. When he was saying the word "launch," he spontaneously raised the hand with the cord over his head, like the commander of a rebel army giving his generals and soldiers a pep talk. The whole crowd started to cheer and whistle again.

Little Yu was among the crowd, craning her neck to get

a better view. Ah-Shui followed Qin Ziqing closely. Little Yu saw some women pointing at Ah-Shui but she didn't feel at all ashamed of her. On the contrary it was natural for Ah-Shui to be in a crowd or to stand beside Qin Ziqing. They appeared a beautiful couple, as if they had been born to be together. Ah-Shan and Gao, Little Yu thought, seemed to be everything but well matched. Luckily they did not see each other much.

As the blowtorch was started, a flurry of excitement spread. The villagers had long wanted to see how the bank notes in the box would fall out when it was cut open. Some of them had bet on the actual amount of funds raised, and the winners would go home with their payouts. Following a shower of sparks the box broke in two with a heavy clang.

What followed, however, was a deathly silence on the square. There was not a single bill in the box, whose ugly mouth faced the sky, as if it had been opened in a brilliant magic show. A throaty roar of murmuring went up from the crowd, and then another.

Rubbing his eyes Qin Ziqing turned to ask Ah-Shui if he was dreaming, only to find she was staring at him with her eyes wide open in shock. He knew she was about to do the same.

Groups of people were swarming into the square. Some of them began to chatter excitedly:

"We saw donors putting money into it, and some did it more than once."

"We still remember how much I gave and how much my neighbors gave. How come it is all gone? Who stole the money?"

"Is Sunny Wuluo a big con? How shameful these con men are to have a blowtorch before us!"

"Don't let them escape! Call the police! Tie them up and put them in jail."

The enraged spectators jumped onto the stage again and again, but were pushed down. There were some guards who were drafted from local banks for security, but now they had to act as armed police, otherwise Qin Ziqing, Ah-Shui and the other committee members would have been killed.

After a search a policeman discovered that there was something fishy about the box itself. He squatted down and with a hammer hit a side wall of the box. A hole the size of a plum appeared after he picked at a spot with his finger. Realizing the box had been tampered with previously, and the hole had been welded shut, he rose to announce, "A hole was already cut into this box!"

The crowd moved their gaze reflexively to the camera installed on a nearby telephone pole. It was covered with a black cloth and dust lay on it in a thick layer. It was obvious the camera had been tampered with days before.

They decided to take the device down for any faint indication of a trail, hoping it had worked under the cover. A ladder was hoisted and a man went up it. He removed the cloth as carefully as he could, only to find underneath was nothing but a small loudspeaker, which was no longer in use. It was even a dirtier trick for which they all had fallen!

It was humiliating to the government officials present, who whispered to one another before the one in the middle rose to announce in a spluttering state of rage, "Effective measures will be taken to investigate and to bring the cheaters to justice."

Then the crowd stormed from their seats in a fit of temper to head to their cars, leaving the emcee standing helplessly at a corner of the stage. The crowd purposefully started to leave without saying a word to Qin Ziqing or even turning their heads to him. However they had all shaken his hand, one after another with a smiling face, before the box was cut open.

"Qin Ziqing will be out on his ass!"

"Nobody will believe a word of what he'll say about it!"

"There you are. Businessmen are businessmen."

His face set and hard, Qin Ziqing turned a deaf ear to the sarcasm. He knew someone was behind it, but it would take time to find out, and today was not the time to do it. The launch date of the project had been chosen with the help of Ma Gu, who had contemplated for a whole night. It was suppose to have been a lucky day and it needed to be a perfect day for the crowd. He couldn't further spoil it now. What he had to do immediately was to put a solution before the audience. Opening the box was simply a prelude to the launch, and an all important item on the agenda was still to come.

However a failed prelude would ruin the whole groundbreaking ceremony. Cracking his knuckles he calculated in his head as quickly as he could the balance of an account. He started from his thumb and then moved to his fingers, producing sharp musical cracks, as if he had an instrument of some kind in his palm. As the sound faded away he finished his mental arithmetic.

He clapped his hands and moved a step forward. He tapped the microphone lightly to see if sound registered before he cleared his throat and spoke into it, "Before we find out who did it, I will auction off my hot-pot restaurant to replace the stolen money. This is now my auction, and I invite the emcee to be my auctioneer to keep track of bids."

The emcee seemed to be deeply touched, and told Qin Ziqing, "You don't have to do it. Think about it. There must be a different way out."

Qin Ziqing answered, "I don't have the time. I need to do what I've decided to do. So now I'm just waiting for the result."

He paused to reflect for a second before he reached out determinedly for the microphone with its red cloth covering. As he gave it to the emcee to use as the auction hammer, he told him his reserve price.

The crowd was completely silenced by how low the starting price was, but the square quickly heated up as bids climbed steadily between bidders. Feeling a rising excitement the emcee loosened his tie, took off his suit jacket, and screamed as if he were one of the bidders.

Suddenly a shrill screaming was heard in the crowd, "Qin Ziqing, you can't do this. The restaurant is mine. Leave it alone!"

The crowd turned their eyes toward the sound, spotting Qin's wife fighting her way to the stage. She grabbed the microphone and threw it hard on the floor, leaving a deafening noise echoing in everyone's ears. She then raised her foot to kick at it and stamp on it, hoping that she could make it stop working so the restaurant would go unsold.

Ignoring his wife, Qin Ziqing thrust a shiny thermos in the hand of the emcee, who took it and raised it high, understanding that he should keep the auction going. The crowd cheered even more loudly.

At twelve o'clock sharp the restaurant reached its reserve, an unreasonably low price, offered by a businessman with an accent. Qin's wife broke down and cried like a baby, "How can I manage without it? What about my son? The whole family lives on it. My heavens! What can we do when it's gone?"

With the auction over the crowd flocked to Cloudy Slope to view the construction site. The project was designed by invited architects and engineers after much discussion. They decided that a large piece of glass in the shape of a fan would be set up on the slope, facing towards the sun to trap as much heat and light as possible, which would then be reflected onto the town in the valley.

An expert builder had been invited days before to put the foundation in place. He had left the previous day and would arrive at the spot again at noon, to finish erecting the panel and unveil it along with Qin Ziqing. They had practiced how to do it at the factory, but the expert warned that nothing should be done until he arrived.

The glass was as high as four to five meters, and the manufacturer had built a good, strong frame to hold it. The panel was wrapped in blankets, and the hoist carrying it trundled along with enough care to prevent any damage while on the road. The foundation had been laid with the help of the expert. A specially designed engine was placed underground by the local electricity company, which would turn the panel slowly westward as the sun moved, in the way a sunflower does. An advertising agency helped with a huge piece of cloth, which was to cover the glass, and a towering scaffolding for Qin Ziqing to use when unveiling it.

After practicing numerous times Qin Ziqing found it a daunting task to pull off the large and heavy cloth with panache. He would have to use all his might and he would have to smile for the cameras. It was a scene he had pictured many times, in which any minor lapse would be disastrous. The Sunny Wuluo project had been under the spotlight for a long time, so he was expecting a great number of reporters, who had never covered anything similar. While the media might consider the project somewhat strange, they believed it was something more pragmatic than to have land cleared in the downtown and cemented to build a square and, therefore, it would be much appreciated.

Villagers swarmed to the spot like colonies of ants, bring life to a slope that was otherwise off the beaten path. Bushes were stamped into the ground and small trees snapped. While adults with babies in their arms picked their way carefully, idle young men and women with pinpricks of sweat along their hairlines struggled to lead, hoping desperately they would be picked out to help.

It was half past twelve when the sun was at its peak, and everything was ready, but the expert was still nowhere to be seen. Looking down the hill nervously the committee members checked their watches for the umpteenth time. The expert should have been with them half an hour before, but the road leading up the hill was empty.

"He might have missed his bus," Qin Ziqing thought, "and in that case we have to wait until tomorrow. What if it rains? Or if it doesn't rain but is misty?" The lost donated money was a severe blow to the project. A delay would surely ruin it.

After considerable discussion, they decided to wait for the expert for another half hour before they attempted to install the panel by themselves. Soon the sun would go down behind the hill, leaving the slope dark and preventing the villagers from seeing how the glass functioned. This, in turn, would lay them open to fresh public skepticism and media criticism.

They had practiced the procedure many times, and they knew theoretically all they had to do was to hoist the glass into a slot using the proper machines. They also said it was not necessary to wait for the expert, because he was only bluffing. He just intended to push himself into the picture to seek personal publicity and claim credit that he didn't deserve. However Sunny Wuluo belonged to the town and the committee, not some expert who just helped in a stage of the process.

Minute after minute slipped by, and the expert didn't show up as they expected. Glancing at his watch for the last time, Qin Ziqing nodded towards his colleagues before he started to climb the scaffolding with surprising agility. Wiping the sweat from his brow, he looked down at the crowd below him. Everyone's eyes were locked on him, their mouth wide open. In front of the crowd was a bank of cameras, which kept clicking, looking like raised rifles aiming at him. Suddenly he experienced a dizzy spell.

With the help of the hoist the glass was installed gradually, "A bit to the left! A bit to the right! Down, down! Slower, slower! Go, go, go! Right there! Good heavens! They slot together! That's so simple. Turn the power on. No hurry. Check it again. Do it again and be sure they are all connected."

The engine started up on the first try. With a nod of his head Qin Ziqing moved to cut the packing tape around the panel, leaving one last thing to do to finish up.

He clenched his fist and let out a long breath before he reached for the red cloth. It seemed he was standing at an awkward angle, so he turned to be in the best position, where he could pull off the cloth in one graceful motion. Looking down he managed a smile for the cameras. It was artificial, but he knew it was necessary, and it might be the last time he was in front of the reporters.

Taking hold of an edge of the covering, he could feel the heat building up on it, as the sun was at its zenith. Making sure that his hold on the cloth was firm enough, he drew in a deep breath and gave it a sharp downward pull. What did he see? His glass, the huge glass, was nowhere to be seen! It was replaced by a small golden hill about the weight of several tons, shining radiantly. He felt a burning sensation in his eyes before everything went black. The pain was so excruciating that he started to scream wildly.

The people on the ground saw him cover his eyes with his hands, cry with pain, and fall off the scaffolding like a floating scarecrow after he released his hold. The glass panel, however, became a great ball of fire on which falling leaves and branches were burning fiercely. The air was quickly heavy with the heady aroma of wood fires.

Villagers who had stayed at home reported that they witnessed the sky lightening up instantly when the panel was unveiled, as if their bamboo door curtains were drawn back. They had to squint their eyes for a few minutes before they adjusted to the brighter light. Soon they began to feel heat building up in the air and they had to take off their coats. For the first time in their lives, they stayed inside with only a shirt on. They all wondered why it had become brighter and hotter.

Qin Ziqing was taken to the hospital. After he had his eyes wrapped in a bandage and his burning body covered with cool creams, he felt a little better and his tight fists unclenched.

With his eyes closed he called Ah-Shui's name as he came to. He was told she had been injured and lay in the neighboring room. He also heard his wife crying in the room.

He suddenly remembered Ah-Shui had been in a place closest to the glass. When he was about to unveil it, his keys came loose from his belt and fell with his sudden movement. She had made her way to the keys, among which was the one to her door. He had heard someone screaming below the glass as he fell down. It must have been Ah-Shui, he dimly recalled.

He felt his way to Ah-Shui's ward. "I can't see you, Ah-Shui," he said.

"Well, it's better that way. You don't have to see how much I've changed. My face was terribly disfigured by the glass."

They didn't speak any more, sitting side by side and enjoying the increased warmth in the room.

"It's really different. It's already six o'clock but it is still brilliantly sunny," she told him.

"It's sad I can't see it," he replied.

"Everyone else can," she continued.

"But they've forgotten us," he said. "I knew they would. There's nothing to do about it. It's how it has always been for me. Eggs are eaten but the hens are seldom remembered."

"But the hens still produce eggs until they are too old to do it."

They were not clinging tightly together, as they had in the past when they were by themselves. They were left alone but they kept each other at arm's length. He didn't speak any more, and she remained silent. He felt a slight chill in the air. She looked out of the window and saw it was getting dark.

"The sun is setting," he said.

"Yes, but it's forty-five minutes later than it was."

She reached out her hand and put it gently on his knee. After a while he raised his to put it on hers.

"You're running a temperature?" he asked.

"You are too," she said.

"Do you regret it?" he asked.

"What about you?" she asked, instead of answering him.

He allowed himself a wry smile. "Maybe I shouldn't have said it was the last thing I was doing for Wuluo. Now it really is the last one. What else can I do if I can't see?"

"No, there's one more thing you can do," she said while leaning to put her arms around him. She did it gently, as he was wrapped in swathes of bandages, with his head injured, his legs in a cast, and one of his arms in a sling. She held him with exaggerated care, as if she were carrying a set of china.

Ah-Shui had a copy of a newspaper in her hand. Rustling it she said in a silky voice, "Tell you what, the story of Wuluo and you has made it into newspapers in the city, in the headlines. They say it's the first time that Wuluo has been in a newspaper report. Unfortunately you can't see it. You look like a hero."

"Pictures of me in the air?"

"Yes, except two of them."

"Do I look ugly in the air?"

"No, not at all. It seems as if you're flying, not falling down."

Qin Ziqing's wife came in with lunch boxes in her hands. She appeared much better now, looking more like a doting mother than the vicious wolf she was in Ma Gu's house. She removed the cover of the box and began to feed her husband. After he swallowed each mouthful, he opened his mouth for the next without knowing where the spoon was.

His wife also had a box for Ah-Shui. When she turned to Ah-Shui, the resigned expression on her face changed to a rare mixture of anger and a smile. Putting the food on her bedside table with a bang, she said to Ah-Shui, "Hey! Look out! I've poisoned the food." With a smile Ah-Shui reached for it and started to eat.

Ah-Shui knew she was not serious. His wife had come to see her when she was first hospitalized. Standing face to face with her, the woman kept silent. Ah-Shui was somewhat fearful, afraid the woman would hit her injured face unexpectedly with her fist, so she bunched her own fingers into a fist, ready to fight. To her disappointment, the woman instead picked up Ah-Shui's coat from where it had fallen on the floor and slammed it on her bed.

Before she left the wife turned and said mockingly to Ah-Shui, "I think it's best for you not to look at yourself in a mirror. At least don't do it now."

Ah-Shui felt an urge to laugh, but with ointment all over her face she managed only a snort of derision. "It saved you a bottle of sulphuric acid. I guess I helped you save money and avoid ending up in jail."

"A woman with her face disfigured is not attractive in a man's eyes," she said.

"But I'm the winner in the end. He will never know what I look like now or when I get old. I'll be the prettiest woman in his mind."

Chapter Seventeen

It was eventually clear who had stolen the money.
Nobody would have suspected Gao if he had not fled.
The day after the large glass panel was installed, Gao simply disappeared and nobody knew where he had gone. At first Ma Gu thought he was just in the bathroom because the basket of radishes he had cleaned was still wet. But he was still nowhere to be found when it was almost noontime. Ma Gu went out to find him, but the neighbors said they had not noticed him. As there was a pot of boiling soybeans awaiting her, she had to hurry home.

Two days passed and Gao was nowhere to be seen. Ma Gu asked Little Yu to report it to the police.

Soon the police arrested Gao, as he and Chun'er had packed up, ready to leave the town forever. He candidly confessed to the crime. He had planned it beforehand. When Chun'er visited the town last time, he had made up his mind to run away with her to a place where no one could find them. She had broken off her engagement to the truck driver, he was unhappy at Ma Gu's snack bar and he had nothing of his own, although it seemed he had everything he needed.

But he needed some money. Where could he go for the money? Ma Gu had some money but he could not get it, as she deposited all her money in the bank and no one else knew the code for her account. He could get nothing even if he killed her. The collection box jumped into his view one day as he was walking down the street with Chun'er. Since then he had been trying to figure out how to open it to take the donations.

After much effort he had gotten the money. At home they spent hours during the night to count it. Much to his disappointment, what he got from the box was only a little more than 2,000 yuan. He said with deep regret that he would have discarded the idea to steal the money if he had known the sum. He earned that much every month at the snack bar, without risking being caught by the police.

The day when he was captured, Ma Gu said to her family, "None of you are allowed to visit him and there will be no mention of his name in the family. Remember we don't know this man." Nobody in the family said anything against this idea.

When she came to the detention center the next day, Gao wailed and whined, almost fainting in front of her, making her red-eyed several times. She said to him, "Behave yourself in jail! You have worked at my snack bar for so long, and I'll pay you for your work. I'll send the money to your parents."

He was still weeping but she turned and left. She had thought about visiting Chun'er but at second thought, she gave up the idea and went straight home.

She had one more important thing to do. She had to ask for some badger fat, the best remedy for healing burns. It was a nagging anxiety to her. She was deeply saddened at the thought of her daughter's burned face; it would be terrible if she was left disfigured for life. But where could she go for the badger fat? Badgers were rarely seen nowadays. She remembered when she was a child each household would keep some badger fat for emergencies.

She was not sure whether her daughter's face would recover one day. She shut herself up in a dark house with a flower in her hand, trying to summon a vision, but she languished days and nights in vain. She began to doubt the miraculous power she had. Or was there no way to help Ah-Shui? If so how could her daughter manage with her terribly burned face? How would she, her mother, be able to manage?

How proud she had been of her two daughters when they had just grown up! They had been like two pretty princesses of Wuluo; wherever they went they would be the center of envy and focus of conversations. All those wonderful days were gone! Although Little Yu, her granddaughter, was quite nice, she was not as well known as her mother and her aunt when they were young. Ma Gu had always thought she could sense an inexplicable kind of bad luck on Little Yu's face. It seemed that this bad luck had been with her ever since she was born.

She asked one shop owner after another about badger fat along the street, but none of them had it, and some had never even heard about it. The more she asked, the more desperate she grew, and the more she believed that it was the only remedy for Ah-Shui's problem.

Suddenly she caught sight of Little Yu, who was hurrying toward the riverside with a bowed head. Ma Gu felt it was strange, asking herself why she would be walking that way when she should be working in the store. She was now interested in her quiet granddaughter with a scarf wrapped around her neck all day long. Following Little Yu silently she wanted to see what her granddaughter was doing.

It seemed Little Yu was wiping away tears. For what reason would such a young girl be so sad? Why did she come to the riverside in grief? Ma Gu decided to put her badger fat mission aside and follow her granddaughter to see what she would do. Close on Little Yu's heels, it suddenly dawned on her that Little Yu had actually grown up. With her tight and round hips, her granddaughter now walked somewhat like a real woman. Letting out a soft sigh Ma Gu knew she had now one more thing to worry about.

It was now dusk. The sunlight reflected from the large glass panel on the Cloudy Slope was fading, and a heavy mist came down. She could see Little Yu's figure moving in the progressing mist. Ma Gu had never before watched her granddaughter so closely. Her buttocks were firm yet they were still a child's; her waist did not sway as a grown-up woman's did; and her hips looked different from her aunt's, which were plump and wiggled as she walked.

Following her granddaughter Ma Gu found herself before Uncle Wang's furniture factory at the riverside. Little Yu hesitated for a while before crouching behind a clump of evergreen bushes.

"Who does she want to see here? Why should she hide herself if she came here to visit Uncle Wang? She has been Uncle Wang's shadow ever since she was a toddler, always on his heels and hips."

Turning to the direction where her granddaughter had fixed her eyes, Ma Gu could also see there was a lit room with nobody in it. She was wondering about it when a growing crack appeared on the wall behind the desk. The gap grew wider until she was astounded to see Uncle Wang coming out of it.

"He can go through the wall! Can he perform magic?" she wondered to herself. She was puzzling about it when a woman followed him out of the wall. Uncle Wang pressed his hand on the wall for a while and the gap closed up after them. Now she understood that it was nothing magical. There was a secret room in the wall for the lovers to meet. Never before had she ever thought that Uncle Wang, who appeared to be an honest man, would have an affair outside his marriage. She saw the woman patting Uncle Wang on the back softly and he answered her with an embrace. The two of them walked out side by side, after the light in the room went out and the entrance was closed behind them.

When she was about to turn around and leave, she saw Little Yu rush up toward them from behind the bushes and throw herself onto him, slapping and kicking.

"Little Yu! Listen to me!" Uncle Wang reached out his hands to try to stop Little Yu regardless of the blows, when she seized his arm and gave it a hard bite. The woman had been on her way to leave but turned back. Uncle Wang waved his hands and glowered at her; she stood there motionless.

Ma Gu seemed to have sensed out something but she could not believe her eyes. "Does it mean that Little Yu and Uncle Wang are …?"

How could it be possible? She had even thought to ask him to be Little Yu's godfather! She saw Uncle Wang free one of his hands to punch Little Yu hard before he could remove his arm from her mouth. He pushed her toward the house yet she resisted. Bending he suddenly picked her up and tucked her under his arm like a bundle of firewood. Regardless of her tumultuous cuffs and kicks, he made his way to the room.

He freed one of his hands to open the door and then slammed it closed after him. Ma Gu followed up to the door. She heard Little Yu howling inside, with Uncle Wang yowling in a deep voice, "Are you nuts? You've bitten me badly. How can I show up in front of people? Why don't you think it over again? How can I muddle along in Wuluo if our affair is made public?"

Ma Gu stood at the door for quite a while. For some time she found herself unable to think clearly. Her head was buzzing and humming as if a machine were running inside it. Little Yu was still wailing. Just as Ma Gu was about to knock at the door, Uncle Wang resumed his speech, "How silly you are, Little Yu. It is out of the question for us to be together in the future. Our affair should never get out.

"Anyway you are a teenager growing up and you will get married. I won't sully your name for anything. I have to ignore you to protect you. Do you really think I want to stay with that woman? I have to do so because I must distract my attention from you to someone else. Otherwise I would have to go after you and that would ruin you. But how can I do that? I could never do that to you. Haven't you ever thought about that? Haven't you realized that I am protecting you that way?"

Little Yu's howl was gradually reduced to continual sobs, just like a water-choked cat, wet and wretched.

Eventually Ma Gu's fingers on the door pressed down and knocked. Inside, Little Yu's sobs were no longer heard. After a while Uncle Wang opened the door. Recovering from his initial surprise, he smiled at Ma Gu. She fixed her eyes upon Uncle Wang. Trying to contain herself, she heard herself say, "I saw Little Yu coming this way and followed her here. I didn't know your furniture factory is right here."

Pretending to be interested in it, Ma Gu followed Uncle Wang to different sections of his factory but she felt her legs tremble slightly. She would not quarrel with him. Making the affair public would bring disgrace to herself, Little Yu and her whole family. She would have to keep it a secret. Little Yu was still so young and there was a long way ahead of her. She couldn't be ruined so early. She would have to keep it to herself to protect her granddaughter. The only way for her to do this was to keep silent and pretend to know nothing about it.

Then she remembered Little Yu, a very young child still, had stayed with her all night when she fainted. She was a good girl and she needed her protection. Ma Gu rubbed her eyes and said to Wang, "Oh, the wet paint stings my eyes."

Bringing her outside Uncle Wang showed her the logs from the remote mountains. Looking at the wood and praising him for his business, Ma Gu suddenly recalled her own husband, who had collected logs on his raft in the river. She could still remember his words, "We'll settle down here in Wuluo. We'll have a large family with lots of kids and they will live here for generations."

Now there were only a few women left in the family, against his expectation. But what could be done about it? She felt terribly sad about it. Ma Gu's tears welled up again. Trying to cover up her feelings, she beamed a smile and said to Wang, "I am very happy to see you're doing so well in your business."

With a little flush on his face, Uncle Wang tried to compose himself yet he still failed to utter a complete sentence.

Ma Gu brought Little Yu back. The moment Grandma had appeared, Little Yu had grown nervous. Drying her tears secretly,

Little Yu pretended to be reading the newspaper while her ears were intent upon things outside. She thought Grandma had discovered something but she quickly dismissed this. It dawned on her that Ma Gu hadn't found out anything special. But she could still sense her grandmother was acting a bit weird—she was holding her hand on the way home, the first time since she was young.

With Little Yu's hands in hers, Ma Gu kept rubbing and massaging them while shedding tears. Little Yu grew upset again and asked her tentatively, "What's wrong with you?"

Taking out her handkerchief to wipe her eyes, Ma Gu said, "Something seems to be amiss with my eyes today and they can't help shedding tears. However I try there is no end to them."

Then she followed with words that scared Little Yu out of her wits, "My girl, we will go nowhere from now on. We, the whole family, will stay at home decently and quietly. There are too many bad guys outside. Can't we stay away from them instead?"

That night Ma Gu cooked Little Yu her favorite food, maize cake, a soft, mellow browned dish with Chinese pickled cabbage and meat stuffing. Ma Gu served it in the nicest tray she had. After the granddaughter finished it Ma Gu grew tearful again.

"Little Yu, my girl, forgive me! I have failed to take good care of you. Both your mother and I failed in this. I will do much better from today on." Moving closer she reached to stroke her hair and scarf, as if Little Yu were a lost kitty regained through much effort.

Little Yu was extremely flattered by her grandma's unusual burst of tender feelings. For several days Ma Gu stayed with Little Yu at night, telling her childhood stories about Little Yu, Ah-Shan and herself and allowing her no time to leave the house. She would go to the bedroom with her granddaughter when Little Yu was sleepy, and plump up the pillow and unfold the blanket for her. When Little Yu fell asleep, she would tuck in the corners of her blanket and lock the door with a clang, before she left reluctantly.

It was a special lock; only Ma Gu had the key to it. It slowly dawned on Little Yu that her grandma was attempting to keep her at home at night, not allowing her out. What embarrassed her most was that she went so far as to throw off her blanket to examine her body. Mumbling some words her grandmother rhythmically stroked her belly and her pelvic bone. She would have nearly reached her private parts if Little Yu had not been quick enough to roll aside.

She said, "Little Yu, you must remember what I tell you. The gift of virginity is the most precious thing a young woman owns. Believe me! I have already renewed your golden virginity. Now you are as pure as when you were born."

Strangely enough, upon hearing her grandma's words, Little Yu felt a wonderful warm feeling come over her, as if she had bathed in hot water. Pulling off her clothes and drawing up her blanket, she was flooded with the happiness of being clean and warm.

The feeling did not last long. Little Yu went to write to Uncle Wang as soon as her grandma left. She must do it; she came to realize that much of what he had told her was a downright lie. For instance he told her that the small room belonged to the two of them, but someone else had been in it. He promised her that he would help in transferring her to a school in the city and pay for her education, but he didn't keep it.

She knew the woman with him in his little room was his secretary. They were colleagues at the factory and could do whatever they liked in the room anytime. Little Yu did not want to compete with the woman. She had something more important to do—she wanted to go to school. She wanted him to keep his promise by paying her tuition fees. It had been because of his promise that she dropped out of school without thinking. She wanted to leave the town with the money and never come back. She would pay no attention to whomever he was with in the secret room.

After finishing the letter, Little Yu thought for a while

before she added one more sentence, "In case you fail to honor your promise, I will come up with some fresh idea and you'll be so frightened that you'll wet your pants." She began to titter at "wet your pants," a phrase that she got a kick out of.

Actually she had no idea what to do to make him "wet his pants." But she knew that she would do something. She had to, if he continued to act like a heartless scoundrel.

On her way to the post office that afternoon, she saw a large number fish floating at a backwater bay along the Wuhe River. Some people on rafts were putting the fish into their bags. She knew that they were using explosives to catch fish. The fish were not wounded but shocked out of their senses by the waves caused by the explosion.

Walking toward a man who was gathering his explosives, she said to him, "Could I have a look at those?"

"Get out of here! What does a little girl have to do with these!"

With his things, the man made his way to a small and low room near water. She knew he was a fisherman and he made a living by fishing. Thinking there must be many explosives in his house, she followed him secretly to his room.

Chapter Eighteen

To everyone's surprise, Sunny Wuluo brought life to the small town.

It all started when tourists with backpacks came all the way to the remote town in twos and threes, asking the way numerous times on their journey. When they finally arrived at the glass panel, they let out a loud cry of astonishment, cheering like naughty kids, before they invited Qin Ziqing for a group photo. Some of them were so excited that they asked Qin Ziqing and Ah-Shui for dinner downtown, where they would drink until they all were tipsy.

More visitors came and the town was turned into a true tourist attraction. The first barrier they had to overcome was the thirty-six continuous sharp turns on either side of the mountain road. It was if they were traveling to Tibet, where some visitors found themselves in a hospital after their plane landed. Those who were not strong enough would be forced to leave the bus, looking pale and vomiting, before they reached the top of the mountain. They would be left with no other choice but to finish the rest of the journey by walking along the twisting asphalt road, making themselves a stick from a tree branch for assistance.

Soon the local villagers hit upon an idea to make money. They offered to carry the tourists in their bamboo pack baskets, which they used for firewood. Most of the visitors were about the weight of a basket of firewood, and the city women were only about forty-five kilos. With a woman in his basket, the carrier would often forget about the weight on his back, drunk on the scent of her strong perfume. They may have previously enjoyed a cable car or a traditional sedan chair at a tourist spot, but it was their first experience in a basket. They cheered wildly like schoolgirls, while their cameras, about the size of half a soap bar, kept clicking. The young carriers were not entirely isolated from the outside world, and they knew the film in a camera needed to be taken out and a new roll loaded. But it seemed that the women on their backs continued to take pictures without putting new film in their tiny cameras. They wondered if they were deluding themselves by pretending to snap pictures.

The first thing the tourists did was to visit Cloudy Slope, where they noisily took pictures of themselves before the glass panel. The local government was quick enough to turn the place into a formal tourist spot by building a small hut near the panel and having Qin Ziqing work there as the guide.

Qin's eyes were still recovering and he wore a pair of sunglasses. With a large scarf over her injured face, Ah-Shui started to act as the ticket seller. Before long they found themselves having to do more work—taking pictures with tourists. They had simply refused all such suggestions at first but later seemed quite pleased to pose with them before the cameras, after seeing the visitors trying to take pictures of them without their knowledge.

They did it because they thought it cost them nothing, but the government men could see in it what they failed to see. The officials had a nice plaque made, and on it they announced that whoever wanted to take a picture with Qin Ziqing, the designer of the project, should purchase a ticket from a different office. They had to pay much more if they preferred Qin Ziqing not wearing his glasses, to show his sunburned eyes, and Ah-Shui not wearing her scarf, revealing her injured face.

Ah-Shui was not happy about it. "I'm not a monkey, you know."

Qin Ziqing tried to persuade her to change her mind, "They don't know who Ah-Shui is and they don't want to know. They take pictures with you, not because you're Ah-Shui but because you're a witness to Sunny Wuluo. They come all the way to our town, and their pictures would be meaningless to them without you and me. They wouldn't be authentic enough, you know? Do them a little favor, okay? Years later when the photo album is open, they will be thinking about Wuluo, the sunless town. Two wise people attempted to make a change but they were injured by the strong sunlight. Even if you live to sixty, what you did here is what will be remembered forever. Your name will be in newspapers, books and part of history. So you'll live longer than anyone else; you will be eternal."

They were encouraging themselves and becoming increasingly interested in the topic of eternity. How many people would be able to live an eternal life? Few ordinary people could, only emperors and their high-ranking generals and officials. They came to realize that to live forever was much more crucial than to live life to the full. Your money didn't last because you would run out of it one day; your love didn't last forever. They talked about the well-known Chinese story in which an old man called Yu Gong moved two mountains in front of his house. Yu Gong was still alive, and he would be alive for all time.

"What about us? Aren't we like him?" Qin Ziqing asked Ah-Shui, full of confidence.

He could not see anything directly in front of his eyes, and was even more far-sighted than he had been. He told her, "My injured eyes are nothing, and your beauty is nothing. Without the glass panel we would age and die. Believe me, even a perfect human body decays. But our project won't. It's part of us. It's like a tree. When we die one day, it will be a small worthless branch falling from the tree, but the tree itself will live forever, for us."

Ah-Shui suggested to her mother that Qin Ziqing come back with her for dinner, but with her head lowered, Ma Gu busied herself, without saying yes or no. Ah-Shui wanted Qin Ziqing to have a good meal, as he had never left the slope since the project started.

With the scarf on her head, Ah-Shui walked along with Qin Ziqing down the hill. The villagers watched them as they headed towards Ma Gu's house. Among them was Qin Ziqing's wife, who stared at them helplessly. Suddenly she cried out, "I've thought it all out. He's something I threw away, something I left on my plate. You take it, I don't give a damn!"

She was not sure if Ah-Shui had heard what she had said, as the expression on Ah-Shui's injured face gave nothing away. Qin Ziqing's expression betrayed nothing of his thoughts either. They walked down the street but it seemed they were flying above the clouds. His wife had a strong urge to repeat what she had said, but she suppressed it after a moment's reflection, as she thought it would draw no response.

Embarrassed she ducked her head and hurried home. She had been busy with her family hotel, created from part of her own house by blocking a door leading to her residence. Everyday she had to serve a few noisy guests, who left early in the morning and returned late at night. It was the huge panel that brought tourists to the town, but when they came they discovered much more than a piece of glass. There were many other things in the remote town that they loved. It was a "rustic farming community," as they called it, which the outsiders had never seen.

The huge influxes of tourists were like swarms of locusts but there was only one actual hotel. Every house was then opened for them, otherwise many of them would have had to spend their nights on the street. With strange faces everywhere around the town, unfamiliar footsteps in each doorway, and unusual clothes hanging from the drying racks on every balcony, Wuluo was no longer a town for locals. It was a different town, where gates and windows had to be left open twenty-four hours a day.

Ma Gu surveyed Qin Ziqing freely, her eyes looking like a

spotlight or those of an owl. She even craned her head awkwardly to see, from the side of his head, how badly his eyes had been injured. Ah-Shui was so embarrassed that she kicked her mother slightly to discourage her.

After waving Ah-Shui out of the door with her, Ma Gu asked, "When will he file for divorce?"

Her daughter replied, "Why a divorce? We're fine—it's best that everyone involved is dealing with everyone else in peace."

The mother's eyes flew open in surprise. "You're not going to get married? So it turns out to be a lot of tears over nothing."

"We'll get married but not now. He told me our wedding would be held when one of us is dying, on the slope."

What she didn't tell her mother was the rest of their plan: After the wedding, they would go into a deep grave with a solid mud arch, which they had been digging secretly for themselves on the slope. At the same time Qin Ziqing had been dictating a short book to her, in which he was to reveal the precise details of his Sunny Wuluo. They would also have the story carved into the walls of their grave.

Qin Ziqing told her that later generations would get to know about Sunny Wuluo, its designers and initiators, and themselves as an unusual couple, when their grave was discovered. He also told her that they should choose to be lovers rather than husband and wife, because lovers had to do with "love" while a married couple was like a piece of fine gauze, which would lose its shape with repeated washing.

It puzzled Ma Gu why the two of them rejected the idea of getting married, as they were together now after the ups and downs they had experienced. She went to Qin Ziqing, intending to ask him accusingly about it, but ended up standing before him in silence. It may have been that he had become a local celebrity or that he seemed unapproachable with his erect seated posture and square shoulders.

Standing quietly for a while, she instead asked solicitously, "Why don't you wear hats? It's hot out there on the slope."

Touching his face with his hand, he said, with his face creasing into a smile, "No, I don't need a hat. My tan is the best promotion of the project."

Ma Gu was slightly surprised to hear what he said. Before her was a man with a tanned face and pearl-white teeth, whose lips were spread in a wide smile as if he were ready to swallow her whole.

Chapter Nineteen

More tourists flocked to Wuluo and the town was overcrowded. As "No Vacancies" signs were seen before all the guesthouses, sleeping bags of all colors were placed along the streets, outside private houses and on paved areas along the Wuhe River. Differing accents were heard everywhere in the town, as if it were a forest where all the birds were singing.

The villagers were all inordinately pleased as the opportunity had finally come for them to get rich. When the heavens close a door, they open a window, they thought. They quickly converted more houses into hotels to make room for tourists, and a street was turned into a gourmet street, where visitors came to enjoy the local specialties.

They thought the outsiders were finally getting to know the beautiful town, which was gradually opening to the outside world, becoming more prosperous day by day. They found themselves among the tourists all day long, selling to them their local foods and cigarettes, and examining their strange but interesting faces. Among them were a lot of foreigners, whom they were seeing for the first time in their lives. To their surprise, visitors from other parts of the world came all the way their small town to appreciate its beauty and to enjoy their foods.

However only a small group of local officials knew that the visitors swooped towards the town, not only for the huge glass on the slope, but for their last view of the scenery along the Yangtze

River, land that would disappear forever before a set date. A hydroelectric dam was being built far away on the river. It was believed to be the largest in the world and, when completed, the water surface would rise more than a hundred meters, in the way that a plugged sink fills with water.

In other words the large area along the river was to become a vast expanse of water, and many cities and villages would be submerged. Many years in the future, scientists would use diving skills and equipment to study the history and culture of their submerged town, as did the archaeologists they saw on television. Therefore the tourists came to the town to witness it before the historical transformation.

Every time the officials walked along the row of hotels, with signboards of all colors, or the street lined with restaurants from which wisps of smoke rose continuously, mixed feelings welled up in them. To them it was nothing short of the last carnival before the end of the world. Everything before their eyes—the buildings, streets, furniture, people, relationships between the villagers—would disappear altogether.

They had been ordered to divide the villagers into groups, who would then be forced to migrate to provinces they had never heard of, like a single clod of dirt, crumbled and spread all over. They knew well that some villagers would refuse to leave the town, but how many of them knew what this meant? When all vanished—their land, grains and houses—they would have no other choice but to move to a new place, learn to speak a new dialect, familiarize themselves with new farmland, crops and seeds, and make friends with new neighbors.

As the water in the Yangtze rose, the Wuhe River was spreading quickly, and it began to abound with fish species that had never been seen. The fishermen were all excited when they saw new fish that were so foolish they had no idea what the fishing net was. They would grab a full load by simply casting their nets, shaking the float lines, pulling them in, and drawing them up.

They had also discovered that the water was rising gradually with a mighty invisible force beneath it, as if a monster in the water were pushing it up while awakening from a deep slumber. This was something they had never experienced in their whole lives. When the government officials came to persuade them they had to leave before the water was too high, they thought the officials were trying to scam them. As locals they knew full well how to deal with the ebb and flow of the tides, as the currents always flowed from upstream to downstream. But this time they were rather frightened as the river no longer functioned like a wok with holes in its bottom—more water was also coming from downstream.

The fishermen's story spread rapidly and it was more convincing to the villagers than the official propaganda. Now they knew that visitors overran their town out of pure curiosity rather than love; they came all that way in order to visit a place that would be submerged soon. A spirit of hopelessness began to pervade the town.

Workers shared what they were facing over the telephone with all those they knew; ignored were the remaining crops in the fields, the fish in the water, and the goats in the mountain pasture. They would not be able to bring them along when they left. They could go with their money but they did not have much of it. Businessmen counted their money everyday and wrapped it up in waterproof plastic sheets before taping it to their body. They believed one had to accept fate, and their money would be with them when they escaped in case of an earlier flood.

The more successful businessmen had worked out their own plans in advance, and Uncle Wang was one of them. He decided upon a new site for his furniture factory when the official migration program was announced. As the deadline approached the villagers were desperately trying to turn everything they had into money, and the prices of wood—logs of pine, chestnut, fir— slumped to their lowest in history. He started his bulk purchase of wood, encouraging all his friends to invest in his plan and borrowing from banks as a "migration entrepreneur."

It seemed he would soon have all the trees in the mountain chopped down and all the logs from the houses collected to ship to his new factory. Even a rough calculation told him that he would make a fortune by simply selling the logs rather than the furniture made from them. While other villagers wore gloomy expressions on their faces, he held his head high confidently. Thinking about his fleet of ships, heavily laden with wood logs on the river, he grew wildly excited. He thought it was a golden opportunity.

Looking at the villagers who wandered along the streets helplessly, he felt a sense of his own superiority. The disappearance of the town would be disastrous for them but it was to be a once-in-a-lifetime chance for him to get rich overnight.

Messages from the first group of migrants were not encouraging. Their families with them and their worthless belongings tied up in a bundle, they had expected a rapturous welcome awaiting them, as if they were friends from afar. Instead they found the people in the new village standing aloof indifferently with no intention to speak to them, letting the strangers know not to trouble them by coming to them for anything. They didn't even prepare water for them to drink. They felt that they were nothing but refugees.

The news irritated the villagers back home who were ready to depart, leaving them feeling a quiet desperation at the future. Their old sayings told them that to settle down in a new place would cost a family ten years, but what they were doing was much more than moving house. They were forced to sacrifice for the country, which deserved, they thought, warm hospitality from the new neighbors. Anyway it was humane to give hungry famine victims food and water when they came for help. Years ago they had moved their cookers out into streets to prepare food for refugees from the flooded neighboring villages. It was a mixture of plain rice and corn, with no vegetables or meat, but the victims were happy because they didn't have to go hungry any more.

The gloomy villagers concluded that Wuluo people have hearts of gold and all strangers have one of stone, but a person with a heart of gold is easily fooled. So from then on their glances at the tourists grew cold and expressionless, and the prices of local specialties rose day by day.

When visitors started to bargain for lower prices, they would shout at them, with tears in their eyes, "That money is nothing to you, but we're losing our homes and we'll be left with nothing." They would then grab the visitors' money from their hands before they could blink.

One day a lonely old man came to Wuluo. He had no guide with him nor did he ask his way. After he got off the ship, he followed the crowd silently to Cloudy Slope. It seemed the place felt faintly familiar to him.

Ah-Shui was telling a group of tourists how the glass had been put into place. Standing alone and away from the glass panel, the old man gazed across the crowd at her. It seemed she was an old acquaintance of his, and he was there to wait for her to finish her work of the day.

The story ended, and Ah-Shui had taken up her bottle to drink when she met the man's gaze. After a cursory glance at him, she focused on her bottle. She drank more than anyone else, and what she drank was not only water but nutritious soup that her mother prepared for her by steeping pork tendon and a medicinal ginseng-like root in water, which was believed to be good for the skin. She gulped down half of her drink when something occurred to her and she turned to look at the man again. The man's eyes were still fixed on her.

"Good heavens! Is it him?" She rubbed her eyes. She then moved nearer and she was sure it was. No doubt. It was no one else but Gao Binghui!

"Heavens. He seems much older than before. He should be. Little Yu's now a grown-up and Ah-Shan has gray hair. It is impossible for him to be as young as before," she thought. When he first arrived he had been in his late middle age and Ah-Shan had just turned into a young woman.

He moved toward her and said, "Now you know who I am, but I recognized you as soon as I saw you."

Ah-Shui stared at him with smile on her face, unable to speak a word.

"I heard about it and saw the picture in a newspaper. I thought it looked like you, but I can't believe it was you," he continued.

Even since she started wearing a large scarf on her head, Ah-Shui was a different woman. After the initial surprise when she met him, she was filled with joy as if he were a long-lost brother. Later she wondered why she didn't blame him and smiled at him without a trace of resentment, while the whole family had almost hated him. Now she understood that maybe it was due to Little Yu, who was after all his daughter. Little Yu had been so close to them, which meant that part of him had been with them for all those years. They were a family, but for some clear reasons they had been separated.

"Ah-Shan ... she ... is everything okay in the family?" he stuttered.

"We're all alive. You haven't seen your daughter for years. She is now much taller, as tall as you. You're here to visit them or for sightseeing?"

He remained silent for a short time, smiling, and then he said, "I have to have a look at this stuff, and then I'll go to them."

He examined the large piece of glass while walking around it. He tried to touch it but withdrew his hand as it was burning hot.

"This is great! Who's the designer? I'm not as clever as that. I think the design is even greater than the device itself. This is a miracle you've created in Wuluo, a miracle no one else has ever created before."

Ah-Shui started to tell him the story of the glass as well as what had happened at the launching ceremony. He told her with regret, "If I were only there. What happened could have actually been foreseen and measures could have been taken."

She replied, "Maybe we should have waited for the expert to come. He's the expert, anyway. But we have absolutely no regrets about it. We did what was reasonable."

Qin Ziqing had heard from Ah-Shui about the story of Gao Binghui and Ah-Shan. Now he reached his hand out to Gao Binghui, who shook it.

"You're making history in Wuluo," Gao told Qin, who answered with a smile. Qin's work at the glass panel had left him with a tanned face from the strong sunlight, and pearl-white teeth, which shone brilliantly under his dark sunglasses. With a sort of dreamy expression on his face, Gao Binghui felt Qin Ziqing very much resembled a blind African American singer in a movie he once watched.

Ah-Shui suggested they go together to see Ah-Shan and Little Yu, but Gao Binghui refused politely, "I'll go alone. I should have done it ages ago."

He then continued, "I didn't want to be away all these years, but I had a lot to deal with. My family has been back there for generations. You must understand the family friends and relationships I have. It was hard work, you know, to manage them when I had to leave for a new place.

"It has been too long but it had to be that long. Some things can be done once and for all but others can't. You have to go through the whole process, with the patience of a saint and in a great deal of pain.

"You see, I'm an aging man. But I'm lucky enough to be able to come back to pay my debt before I die. I thought I would never come back to do it.

"I'm not sophisticated enough to live a double life. I start a new one only when the other ends. That was the reason why I left Wuluo. I could never manage a life involving two women. I rather admire those people who handle an even more complicated life. I tried to do the same but every time I made a terrible mess of my life."

Ah-Shui was puzzled by what he told her, but she was sure he wasn't lying or making up some excuse for his return. She had known almost nothing about him, but it seemed that this brief conversation helped her to gain access to his inner life.

Gao Binghui walked down the hill alone. Ah-Shui stood gazing at him from behind. Instead of gaining weight, he was slightly slimmer. She thought that he had once been like a shady tree in full leaf but now stood with only bare branches. She felt a sudden pang of bitterness.

She noticed a flashlight was dangling from his pack. Since he had lived in Wuluo for some time in the past, he must have thought the town was still covered with heavy mist, and that even before it was getting dark he would be able to see nothing a meter away. She had the urge to go home by way of a shortcut to tell her family the news before he arrived, but she checked herself after a few steps of running.

"I don't have to be in such a hurry. Ah-Shan has waited for nearly half of her life; a few more minutes are nothing to her."

Trying to suppress her excitement, she walked slowly towards Qin Ziqing. Weakly pressing his arm around her waist, he said. "I have a hunch that Gao Binghui won't leave any more. He'll stay with Ah-Shan and Little Yu in the town."

"How do you know?"

"I'm a man, and I surely know how a man thinks."

Chapter Twenty

Gao Binghui walked unhurriedly down Cloudy Slope to the Gaoshan Snack Bar by the river. Nothing around was how it had been. The river was narrower with slower water. The narrow street had been expanded and repaved, concrete replacing the slippery, wet stone slabs. The gardenias with their heady scent were nowhere to be found on windowsills and in wall cracks.

In the distance Gao saw the sign for the snack bar, wondering why the name had been chosen and why it contained the character "Gao." Did it have something to do with his surname? It was not hot, but he had to wipe the sweat from his brow.

He saw a woman throwing slops onto the street. She was stooped, with gray, uncombed hair on her head as if she wore a hat made of snowflakes. When he recognized the woman was Ma Gu, he suddenly remembered what she had told him, "Please don't come again to trouble my daughter. She hasn't seen much of the world, and she isn't able to get up and begin again if she falls."

He had tripped her and sure enough she had never gotten up again. All of a sudden he was wondering what to say when he met them. He had to calm himself down as he was too nervous to recall what he had prepared for the meeting.

Then a commotion was heard, and the people in the street were running in one direction. He heard a voice over the noise, "Go and look. Something terrible is happening! It's Little Yu, the granddaughter of Ma Gu. She is on Uncle Wang's freighter with a belt of explosives around her waist."

Gao was taken aback, wondering, "Is she my Little Yu?" He was quickly caught up and joined the stream of people.

A cargo ship was anchored at the quay. On its deck were piles of logs, making it seem as if it were an aircraft carrier. Recently fleets of ships heavily loaded with passengers or cargo had become a common scene at the river. While the people were carried upstream, the cargo was unloaded in the town. As the whistles kept hooting, the water was becoming muddier and darker.

On the large ship, before a high pile of wood, stood a man and a woman. The woman wore a bluish short-sleeved shirt, white pants and a green scarf around her neck. She was as slight and weak as a pre-teen, and her bare arms were thin and smooth. She stood on the gangplank with her feet apart, seeming to willfully stand in the way of the robust middle-aged man who was about to leave the ship. He had a suitcase in one hand and he kept waving his other hand in the air. His voice was stifled by the strong wind so it was impossible to interpret what he was saying. But it appeared he was wildly excited.

Gao Binghui elbowed his way quickly towards the front of the crowd. He saw that few people were standing near the water, afraid of being at the front of the crowd. The young woman had a belt of explosives around her waist, threatening to light it. Upset, the man was screaming at her, but she stood speechless and expressionless. He was leaving the ship but she stood in his way on the gangplank. It seemed she was ready to strike the detonator in her hand anytime, which would be profoundly disastrous.

Gao Binghui walked slowly into the shallow water with his shoes on. As he moved forward he recognized the young woman: it was his daughter, Little Yu. Her eyes resembled his exactly while her nose and mouth were very much like Ah-Shan's. Tears were falling on her cheeks, and her hair was wet with tears and sweat. Distantly he could hear what they were saying.

"You're a liar. You lied to me from the start. How could you do it? You know I hate liars. My mom was screwed, and you've been screwing me."

"Listen, Little Yu. That man lied to your mom but I've never lied to you. I've been struggling to keep afloat. I'm in the wood business, and I would have even pawned my undershorts for money to buy wood. I've borrowed from many people and banks. I'm heavily in debt. Why can't you wait? Why can't you give some consideration?"

"You've been lying. You promised to give me the money when you celebrated the anniversary of your factory but you failed. You told me you would do it when your goods sold, and you broke your promise again. I know what tricks you're playing—I'll never see you again after you move your factory, and then you can get away without paying what you owe me."

"Little Yu, it's not right to say this in front of everyone. What do you mean that I'd get away without paying you? I owe you nothing. Why should I pay you?"

"I'm not lying. You promised me the money but you broke your promise. That's my money. Come on. You can never leave without paying off the debt."

"When did I borrow from you? I have a big factory, and I borrowed from a girl?"

"You want me to reveal it all? Don't think I won't do it. I don't even fear death now, so do you think I would try to save face?"

Uncle Wang reached his hand out, to stop her from saying what she was going to say. "Ok, Little Yu, let's say I owe you the money. But you're standing in my way. How can I get the money for you? I need to leave the ship to do it."

"Let's stop playing games. Why don't you ask your secretary to do it? She does whatever you say, doesn't she? She's with you day and night, isn't she? Tell her to come with the money for you. You are not going to get out of here unless you give me the money."

"She doesn't have the money nor do I. I don't have the money to pay for this shipment of wood. I've told you I'm now deeply in debt, and I need to make furniture with the wood to earn a profit, you know. I tell you what, I'll give you an IOU and it will mean I owe you the money. Okay?"

"No, no, no! You must pay me in cash here and now. I'll never come to you to claim an IOU. Do you think I'll come to you again? You're wrong, you filthy pig."

"Well, you're using nasty words. Why didn't you do that when you were dying to be with me?"

"Are you giving me the money or not?" Little Yu said in a threatening tone while making a motion toward the ring in her hand. Uncle Wang was immediately silenced, fearing that she would trigger the explosive with a simple pull. They halted their quarreling, standing still.

It was boiling hot and everyone's forehead was dripping sweat. Seeing nothing was happening, some in the crowd were growing impatient, "Hey, are you going to pull on the ring? It seems you've got to think it over, so should we come again after dinner?"

Gao Binghui had a strong urge to call her name, but he suppressed it, fearing she would be too excited to see him and set off the explosive by mistake. He stood wordlessly in the water, feeling helpless as to what to do to help her out of the danger.

"Believe me, Little Yu. I'll give you the money soon, and I'll find you a school beyond the mountain. I mean it. Believe me, and I'll give you the new address of my factory and you can come for me. You believe I'm sincere, don't you?"

"You're up to things again. You can never cheat me now. I know you're a liar and a dirty man. I trusted you so much but you lied to me. I hate liars more than anything else."

"I've promised you the money but you keep calling me a liar?"

"That's what you are. You told me the room was for me. Then why did you have other women in it? Tell me how many women you've been hanging around with. Why did you lie to me? Why did you promise me? You thought I would be easily fooled?"

She started to cry while continuing to speak between sobs, leaving Gao Binghui wondering what she was saying.

"Well, well, Little Yu, you're not a teenager any more. Why didn't you see I did all that for your own good? I tried to protect you. It's good for you if I leave you alone. I know you don't believe me, but you'll understand all my efforts when you're older and you'll see I did it for your benefit."

"Shut up! You're lying. I'm not easily fooled any more. I've found you out at last, you cheat! You make big promises but you have no intention of keeping them. Give me the money right now. You are trying my patience! I'm not going to stand for any more of your nonsense."

"Little Yu, you young bitch, think about how kindly I treat you," shouted a woman coming up from the crowd, "but you're threatening my husband. I don't fear death, either, and I'll fight it out with you."

She was running towards the gangplank, but stopped in the middle to hurl verbal abuse when she saw that Little Yu stared at her in anger, ready to pull on the ring in her hand.

Little Yu let out a sudden contemptuous laugh. "Good. I'll kill one more. Come on, you two. I'm alone but you're a family. Two for one is a good deal. Come on. You and him. Don't be afraid."

The two adults were frightened. After a while Uncle Wang told his wife in a resigned voice, "You go home for ten thousand yuan. Let's say I've made a loss on a deal. I can't waste my time any more; time is money, you know."

"We should pay her so much? For what? How did she trip you up?"

"I promised to help her go to a school in the city."

"Why did you do that? You're not her father."

"Don't talk nonsense! Do what I said. All you women are the same. All you care about is money."

He shot a contemptuous glance at Little Yu, who snorted with a long face. The woman looked at her husband and then Little Yu before storming off in a huff.

After a few steps, she returned to ask, "Well, it still puzzles me why you have to pay her a bundle. Are you having an affair with her? Tell me the truth about it before I go for the money."

"Ask him about it. He knows everything about it," Little Yu said.

Her husband looked away, ignoring both of them.

Little Yu told his wife, "You're puzzled? Actually you know what happened between us but you've been lying to yourself. I'll tell you now that what you're suspecting is what really happened—and more."

The woman stood in shock for a second before she pounced on Little Yu with a despairing cry. Frightened, Little Yu unconsciously moved back. The woman nearly got hold of Little Yu when Uncle Wang jumped to his feet. He was ready to escape while the two women were wrestling with each other, but Little Yu made a sudden dive for his sleeve.

All of a sudden, the three of them were in a clinch. Gao Binghui heard a muffled voice saying, "I don't want to live any more." Then the explosive blew up with a deafening noise, leaving him deeply unconscious. It happened so suddenly that no one knew who pulled the ring.

Gao Binghui found himself lying on the beach when he came to, soaked through with muddy water. He squirmed on the ground before he sat up slowly, suffering from severe pain in his leg, which dribbled blood. On the ground around him were spots of blood. Looking up to the river, he saw the wreckage of the cargo ship aground in shallow water. The pile of wood was reduced a few dozen stray logs, from which stripped tree bark dangled, showing spots of pale wood.

Not a single person was seen around. He suddenly started to wonder whether he had woken from a dream or had something really happened. Before he answered his own question, he fell into a faint again.

A few weeks later, he was in Ma Gu's house at a strange family meeting. Ma Gu sat at the head of the table, with Qin Ziqing and Ah-Shui on one side of her, and Gao Binghui and Ah-Shan on the other side.

Ah-Shan had recovered fully from her nightmarish daze, which had lasted for nearly half of her life, after Little Yu was buried. It may be that she was moved from it by her daughter's death or by Gao Binghui's return.

On that day, after hearing everyone in the street shouting at the top of their voices about Little Yu, Ah-Shan had run dreamily to the river where she suddenly caught sight of a man covered with blood, struggling to get to his feet. Just as she was averting her eyes from him, something dawned on her and she let go of the small basin in her hand, which rolled down a slope to the river. She called out "Binghui" and started to walk towards him unsteadily, as if in a trance. Stopping before him she stood in silence. She was not reaching out her arms for him, but tears blurred her vision.

He stood motionless, too, gazing at her. She was no longer the gorgeous young woman he knew, but the way she looked at him was exactly as it had been—her eyes were as brilliant and filled with longing and desire. Age had left no trace in her eyes. When she snapped back from her memory of the past, he stretched out both his arms. Slowly she fell into them and he reeled backwards.

She had not thrown herself into his arms. She had fainted.

The first thing Ma Gu noticed when Ah-Shan revived was her daughter's eyes, which were as bright as they used to be. "My older daughter's back!" she murmured.

With her eyes fastened on her mother, Ah-Shan kept smiling. The way she smiled, the look on her face, and even the way she curled her mouth had all changed. She was a different person now!

She turned to Gao Binghui with a smile. "I knew you would return. I always dreamed it. Once you wept in my dream, sobbing alone in your office, and I understood you were missing Wuluo."

He just nodded mutely. He had become speechless, unable to speak a word in front of her ever since their reunion. Blankly but amorously, his eyes trained on the woman. She had changed physically but he could still see the same Ah-Shan, and he was left to wonder where he was now. His memory suddenly failed him as to where he had traveled, where he was, and why he was where he was. He had lost all his memory, as if he was under a magical spell, his brain addled by how the woman gazed at him, unable to do anything but focus his eyes on hers.

With all other things done, the first-ever family meeting was to be held in the house to discuss, rather formally, several important issues. The much-reported dam beyond the mountain was about to be completed. Soon the town of Wuluo would be submerged. A local official had visited Ma Gu numerous times to discuss when her family would move to the new place, but in vain. What she told him was always the same, "You go and tell the children to leave, but I will stay. My days are numbered. I won't leave for any place. I prefer to be drowned by the rising water."

The official was upset and rose to his feet. "I'd be shirking my duty if you refuse to leave. You know, you're old but why don't you do me favor? I will be fired if you don't."

What he said upset Ma Ga. "Tell your superior officer to visit me. You two can watch how I die in the water, and you won't be shirking your duty."

When the official left, Ma Gu came to feel sorry for him after mulling it over, and hit upon the idea of a family meeting.

Ma Gu was the first to speak at the meeting, "You move to wherever you like but leave me alone. I'm old and I'll die sooner if I leave. It's best for me to stay and to be with your late father and Little Yu in our own village."

With Qin Ziqing's hand in hers, Ah-Shui said, "We'll also stay. We have to be with our glass. We're nothing but two ugly creatures without it. We're different when it is nearby. We won't go anywhere unless we leave with it."

Ma Gu seemed to disagree. After an initial silence she raised her head to look at Gao Binghui, enunciating each word of hers clearly and carefully, "I have a favor to beg of you. Leave here with Ah-Shan. Be nice to her and she'll enjoy a life of two people in love."

Ah-Shan cut in, "I won't leave, I'll stay where you are. I'll be with you. I would die without you."

"Listen. One of us must struggle to live on. And for the sake of Little Yu, you have to go. She longed for a school in the city. You go, and she'll go. Her soul will leave with you."

Gao Binghui said, "I had intended to stay so I dealt with everything before I returned here. I came to stay. Well, I'll give in and stay with Ah-Shan."

The meeting lasted as long as half a day, marked with laughter and tears. It was declared closed with Ma Gu's decision, "I say that Ah-Shui should stay and Ah-Shan leave. Go and pack up for tomorrow's ship."

Ah-Shui nudged Ah-Shan out of the room and helped her pack. Ma Gu ran her fingers through her hair and left without saying anything. She had one last thing to do before Ah-Shan left—to marry off her two daughters in her own way. She was well aware that what she was planning went against the local custom, as neither of the daughters had an official marriage certificate. The whole town was to be underwater; where could they go for it? But it was her last wish, something she longed for all her life. She had imagined many times what her daughters' wedding ceremonies would be like, even when they were little girls. To cry at a wedding was a local custom, but Ma Gu knew that these lamenting marriage songs varied from one bride to another. She had thought about what songs she would choose for Ah-Shan and Ah-Shui years before when she planned to marry them off. However she had never been given the opportunity.

To her surprise it seemed her wish would come to nothing. With their household belongings and farm animals and pets, the last group of emigrants was sitting by the river in distress, waiting for the transport ship to come. Some of them carried on their backs a tree from beside their house. The streets were empty of people. Most villagers had gone, and Ma Gu was wondering where she could find a group of young women to perform the traditional lamenting. It was the last day for them in their hometown, and everyone was filled with gloom and depression, making it impossible for her to invite even a single guest to the wedding. To make things even worse the trumpeters had left, leaving only one gunman who could fire a salute.

Ma Gu had no other choice so she decided they would manage it all by themselves. She told her daughters that she had been a great singer when she was young.

When the sun was in the west, Ma Gu started her work in the kitchen, beginning to cook the finest specialties of the house, a supper that her daughters would remember all their lives. Wearing their best clothes, her daughters helped her. The ceremony started while they cooked, and Ma Gu was first heard singing:

> There are many stars but no moon
> You'll be an enormous worry to your parents
> They fear you would go hungry
> They fear you would be ill
> They fear you would have to be in rags
> They fear you would be unlucky—

Her daughters continued:

> You have a bridal veil covering your head

Your brothers and their wives go after you to
  your home
Other parents with sons are getting rich
But ours have been left with nothing
They're heartbroken as you're leaving—

Suddenly three gunshots were heard. It was Gao Binghui firing a triple-barreled gun that he had borrowed. He charged the gun with an explosive powder and then rammed in a long iron rod to tamp it down before he lit the fuse and put the cover on. He performed the process as if he were an experienced gunman.

Something strange happened when they turned to look at the moon. It was opening like a Chinese cabbage whose leaves were about to burst, leaving a much brighter sky. Standing on the roof of the building, the five of them remaining in the family saw before their eyes the deserted town with its empty houses, desolate streets, and lonely hill slopes. Everything was eerily quiet, aside from the sound of running water in the distant Wuhe River.

Her eyes fixed on the river, Ma Gu noticed that the water had almost submerged an enormous bead tree whose roots had been out of the water just yesterday. The dam had been breached, and the water was running wildly into farms, fields and ditches. Ma Gu suddenly turned to her family and said, "Actually our Little Yu was nothing short of a genius. She concluded the Yangtze River was like a centipede when she was a little girl. Look, the Wuhe River also looks like a centipede."

The family commenced to memorialize the dead Little Yu.

"She had never seen a dragon, and what she knew was a centipede. She was too honest to say anything that she was not sure of. She was totally honest all her life."

"She told me, 'Neither Wuluo nor the Wuhe River is big enough to be shown on a map. It is the same with people; I'm not big enough and I'm not wanted.' I asked, 'By whom?' But she didn't answer me. She was a silent girl but she thought more than children of her age."

It was midnight and the large ship for the emigrants was about to leave. Standing on the shore, Ma Gu, Ah-Shui and Qin Ziqing watched from a distance as Ah-Shan and Gao Binghui waved their hands from the deck.

"Look, they seem like husband and wife standing shoulder to shoulder," Ma Gu said with tears in her eyes.

"What are you talking about? They are husband and wife," Ah-Shui replied.

"What I mean is they haven't seen each other for more than ten years, but they're as much a match as they were when they met."

"I guess my sister was pretending. She put herself in cold storage as soon as Gao Binghui left but when he returned she melted in no time. You see, they look as they were."

As the gangplank was coming up, Ah-Shan began to weep. The way her daughter screamed out "Mom" reminded Ma Gu of Ah-Shan as a baby, when she was hungry and wanted to be nursed at her mother's breast. All of a sudden Ah-Shan turned to run downstairs and then along the corridor on the first floor.

"Oh, no! She'll jump from the deck!" Ah-Shui cried out. In no time Ah-Shan was on the gangplank and then plummeted to the water.

Luckily the water was shallow and she was able to get hold of a log after some struggling. And then a splash was heard. It was Gao Binghui, who had jumped into the water and was swimming toward her.

"The ship won't stop for you. You'll regret it," she said.

Gao Binghui remained silent but his eyes filled with sudden tears.

"Binghui, think what we're doing and tell me if it's great love between us."

The tears rolled down his cheeks. With his arm around her waist, they walked to the sandy shore. The gangplank was now back in place, and the ship turned slowly and moved away gloomily.

The next day Ma Gu and her family moved to Five-Peak Mountain, into a transportation post that had been deserted for years. One morning several days later, she was shocked when she looked down in the direction of Wuluo. She cried out, "The town vanished!"

It did disappear, leaving a couple of hills struggling to keep their heads above the boundless water. They looked as if they were just peeking through.

Had the town vanished from the earth? It had!

Looking at one another, none of them was able to speak.

Stories by Contemporary Writers from Shanghai

The Little Restaurant
Wang Anyi

A Pair of Jade Frogs
Ye Xin

Forty Roses
Sun Yong

Goodby, Xu Hu!
Zhao Changtian

Vicissitudes of Life
Wang Xiaoying

The Elephant
Chen Cun

Folk Song
Li Xiao

The Messenger's Letter
Sun Ganlu

Ah, Blue Bird
Lu Xing'er

His One and Only
Wang Xiaoyu

When a Baby Is Born
Cheng Naishan

Dissipation
Tang Ying

Paradise on Earth
Zhu Lin

Beautiful Days
Teng Xiaolan

The Most Beautiful Face in the World
Xue Shu

Between Confidantes
Chen Danyan

She She
Zou Zou

There Is No If
Su De

Calling Back the Spirit of the Dead
Peng Ruigao

White Michelia
Pan Xiangli

Platinum Passport
Zhu Xiaolin

Game Point
Xiao Bai

Memory and Oblivion
Wang Zhousheng

Labyrinth of the Past
Zhang Yiwei

No Sail on the Western Sea
Ma Yuan

Gone with the River Mist
Yao Emei

The Confession of a Bear
Sun Wei